MW01016500

The Treasure
of
Blackbeard's Island

DIANA LYDIA HOHLACHOFF

Copyright © 2014 by DIANA LYDIA HOHLACHOFF

All rights reserved.

Cover illustration:
A Wherry Taking Passsengers out to Two Anchored Packets,
an 1825 painting by Scots artist William Anderson (1757–1837),
available as a public domain image from Wikimedia Commons.

Copy editing, book design and typesetting by Erik Pedersen.

ISBN 9781495204555
Printed in Canada

Contents

1.　I sail in search of fortune

I, CHRISTOPHER BERKSHIRE, take up my pen in the year of our Lord July 1, 1759, forty years to the day after embarking at the tender age of 12, to relate my story of the treasure of Blackbeard's Island and the various incidents that transpired on that fateful high-seas voyage of discovery, intrigue and whirlwind adventures. Captain Salisbury and the crew of the *Vigour* were charged with the task of seeking booty hidden by the infamous Blackbeard, one of the most notorious pirates ever to sail the seven seas.

My father was originally from Reading, but had moved near Stoke-on-Trent to assume ownership of the White Horse Inn, a lodging establishment operated for some years previously by my maternal grandfather, though my grandparents had died before I was born. Before my father, too, passed away some years later, I had fond memories of being dandled on his knee by the hearth and of being carried about on his shoulders on occasional tramps through the countryside.

After my father's passing, my mother took on the burden of operating that inn as her means of livelihood. I had only a little formal education, enough to read, write and do sums. I had to leave school before beginning the study of Greek or Latin, let alone the astronomical navigation, botany, French or Spanish that might have been helpful to me on my future voyages.

I first met with Captain Salisbury after he had fallen into conversation with my mother whilst staying at her establishment for two nights. He was on his way to Liverpool to outfit his ship, the *Vigour*. He intimated at that time that he had need of a cabin boy to complete his seafaring crew.

I was of a rather wiry, slight build, yet strong in the arms from waiting on table carrying endless mugs of warm beer to the regular patrons and newly arrived travellers from London, Birmingham, Manchester, Leeds and other parts of the country serviced by the King's Highway.

My mother agreed to my apprenticeship as a cabin boy after Salisbury observed that my younger brother Ned was now strong enough to wait on tables. He also paid a small sum to my mother for my indenture. The captain and his officers under him were to train me, an innkeeper's son, in the ways of our seafaring nation.

After lengthy conversation, my mother and the good captain Salisbury had discovered that he was a distant relative, a third cousin once removed from my father's side of the family (a rather tenuous connection, to be sure). Still, my mother insisted that I be treated as a family member because of my young and tender years, a suggestion to which the captain readily acquiesced, promising to treat me as if I were his own son or nephew.

The captain had a most kindly countenance, and his twinkling aquamarine eyes bespoke an obvious good nature. He was fortyish, about six feet tall with a somewhat muscular build, though his lean frame made him appear younger than his years. His demeanour commanded firm authority, yet he seemed ever kind, with a look of pleasantness that shone through his slightly uneven, toothy smile.

I remember how he patted my head after my mother introduced me as her precious, eldest son. My father had been taken from us in a bout of consumption seven years before. We had been in dire straits subsequently, due to his unfortunate and untimely passing from this world. My mother had had to assume most of the work of running the inn, and Ned and I had gradually taken over more tasks as well. Salisbury assured my mother that I would receive the best possible care. Mother was continuously worried about my health and blessed me profusely when I sneezed or coughed, even if it was just from the smoky fireplace, from the redolent stink of a mutton-tallow candle or from Cook spilling goose fat in the kitchen hearth while preparing pub fare for our guests. It was a constant worry to Mother, since she did not wish me to succumb to the fate that had befallen my father.

I was to accompany the captain and his crew on this adventure on the high seas as his personal cabin boy, later to be trained as a ship's officer. Captain Salisbury and my mother drew up the terms of my apprenticeship, a plan which suited me well, as I wished to pursue a life of adventure after my rather uneventful childhood in the small English village of Middlewich. I would miss my mother with all my heart, but I knew no other way of aiding her in her dire need.

Salisbury had met this morning with the officers of his ship, the *Vigour*, to set a course for our journey and to establish the terms under which his partner, a Mr. Harcourt Derwynn, had underwritten this voyage to seek buried treasure on Blackbeard's Island, he being firmly convinced that the piratical Blackbeard had hidden untold wealth and treasure there. The captain, along with his senior officers, had painstakingly drawn up plans for a four-month voyage on the *Vigour* in hopes of recovering treasure beyond our wildest dreams.

The infamous Edward Teach, known as Blackbeard because of his thick black beard tied up with lengths of red ribbon, which he supposedly set afire in times of combat and engagement to strike fear into the hearts of his opponents, had just been killed in battle off the Carolinas the previous year.

Salisbury told us how Blackbeard's ship, the *Adventure*, had been grounded in shallow waters. The brave and determined Lieutenant Maynard had refused to allow the notorious pirate to steal his own ship, the *Jane*, shooting him at close range with his pistol. Blackbeard, however, kept fighting, despite his wound. When the Lieutenant's sword broke, he was saved by a Royal Navy sailor, a Scotsman whose swordsmanship finally got the better of the notorious pirate scourge. With a single swipe of his broadsword, the sailor had stopped the fight, slicing off Blackbeard's head. After a few more pirates had been killed, the remainder of their number had surrendered.

Lieutenant Maynard had then repaired his two ships, the *Jane* and the *Ranger*, and sailed for Williamsburg, Virginia, with Blackbeard's severed head dangling from the bowsprit of the *Jane*. In Williamsburg, Governor Spotswood saw to it that the

13 captured rogues were convicted of piracy and hanged. Even before Blackbeard's slaying and the capture of his crew, there had been stories of hidden pirate booty, and Captain Salisbury was optimistic that the voyage Mr. Derwynn had commissioned would succeed and that we would be able to bring the fabled, ill-gotten treasure home to England.

Our voyage commenced after much fanfare and many long, tearful farewells. The wives and loved ones of the crew — children, grandmothers, grandfathers and people of every age and description — spent their last tearful moments on the docks together. Young children clung tearfully to their fathers as their mothers gently pried them away. These men were from all sorts of backgrounds, from seasoned mariners to ploughboys plucked right from nearby counties. They wished to sail to far-off lands in hopes of returning with great fortunes to retire in the English countryside as captains of industry or lords of vast estates. None had been shanghaied or otherwise pressed unwillingly into service. My mother joined the throngs of well-wishers for a safe, prosperous and speedy journey home.

"Goodbye, Mother," I said sadly. "I'll sorely miss you."

"I will miss you too, my son, my own!" Her lower lip quavered, and I think she must have feared she would never set eyes on me again. With youthful exuberance and optimism, I assured her I would soon return. "I shall pray for your swift return. My heart is with you always, across all the seas and continents of the world," she continued, her eyes now brimming with tears and her voice quaking with strong emotion. "I'll keep you in my heart always, as you and Ned are the dearest to me in this world."

No longer able to contain them, tears began to well up in my eyes as well, as I embraced her once again. "I shall return as soon as I can, Mother."

"Godspeed, my love," Mother said. I feared her heart might burst on the spot, since we had never before been apart for more than two days at a time.

Gently and sadly, I extricated myself and clambered up the gangplank of the three-masted brigantine with my heavy duffel bag and, I think, much of the weight of the world on my still-narrow, young shoulders.

She watched me board the *Vigour* and cast me one last longing look before I waved to her and followed another sailor as we climbed down a hatch and disappeared into the ship's hold to find our bunks and stow our gear.

She had left the coach-stop, knowing that the driver would return in two hours' time to return her to the White Horse Inn in Middlewich, the only home I had ever known. In my mind's eye, I imagined her turning heel to hail the coach bringing her back to our inn, and though I already missed her grievously, I could not help but look with excitement on the adventure to come. I little knew at the time that it would be the last I would see of my mother for a very long time.

The bustle of the crew members on the *Vigour* soon took my mind off my mother and our financial woes. Our public house was still mortgaged to a humourless and unpleasant former partner of my father. Though the inn was flourishing because of its location close to the main King's Highway, my mother was still heavily indebted and at the mercy of this so-called gentleman of dubious reputation. I would have to redress this situation myself with this voyage and all its ensuing perils at sea, whatever they might turn out to be.

Barrels of salted and dried beef, fish, rum and wine were stlll being rolled up the wide, rough-hewn planks onto the ship whilst awaiting transfer to the stores deck. Flocks of hens, six goats and even a herd of pigs were brought aboard and penned behind the ship's wheel to provide fresh eggs and meat on the voyage. Large wooden boxes filled with tackle, blocks, chains and lines were hauled up by rope and pulley and then guided inside. More provisions were still being yarded onto the decks, already piled high with much-needed supplies for the long voyage. Numerous crew members rolled barrels and barrels of fresh water up gangplanks and onto the ship, and the men's braids and curls flew about with the effort of their work.

I learned later that today's frantic activity was only the last day of a fortnight of ship's lading; it takes a long time, indeed, for the chandlers and longshoremen to adequately supply such a vessel for its sea voyage.

Mr. Sullivan, the first officer, shrilly blew a ship's whistle for a sustained time. "All ashore that's goin' ashore, and all men on board that's goin' aboard!" he ordered.

"Mr. Swanson?" he inquired a short time thereafter. "Are all the men present?"

"Aye, aye, sir!" replied the boatswain. "All present and accounted for."

"Then make ready to sail, bos'n."

"Make ready to hoist the mains'l," ordered the leather-faced boatswain.

The crewmen scurried up the rope ladders with the dexterity of monkeys and the skill of years of experience at readying the ship's sails.

"Trim the mizzen and the jigger, and be smart about it," continued the boatswain, as the wind began to catch the *Vigour*'s array of sails. The swell of the ocean was increasing, but the westerly wind was still light.

I had not noticed this on previous journeys to the busy harbour, but I now became aware of two longboats that, manned with strong, able-bodied sailors, were towing the *Vigour* out of port so that our ship's sails would be able to catch the offshore winds. I learned later that this was a fairly common practice, as there was less wind in the protected harbour and it avoided risk to both the ships and the docks if a sudden gust were to catch a ship's full canvas. On the other hand, if the winds were favourable and particularly strong, the crew would have to row double-time for the piloting longboat to catch up to their ship so as not to be left behind.

As the longboat oarsmen slowly manœuvred the *Vigour* out of port, a strong gust of wind did catch her fore-and-aft staysails and the longboatmen hauled themselves up ropes onto the deck of the ship. They were finally underway for the first lap of their journey to Blackbeard's Island, having set sail later than expected due to a delay in the arrival of a further supply of dried salt beef. The mariners broke out into rousing sea shanty, glad to be on their way at last.

The men on deck set about their duties righting the rigging and trimming the sails. At eight bells, as was the custom, they congregated on the deck for their daily draught of rum, carefully measured out and poured into their pannikins.

"Well, Mr. Miller," said the quartermaster to the lead seaman, "shall we see who shall predict the day and hour when we drop anchor on this here Blackbeard's Island? The winner will have the first opportunity to choose any trinket from the treasure we find." The two fell to good-natured discussion, but as they were now speaking in more hushed tones, I once again returned to the captain's quarters to fulfil my cabin boy duties.

Within a few days, I had become accustomed to the ship's routine. What surprised me the most, especially after having noted the great quantities of supplies and the full complement of mariners engaged to sail her, was the rather small size of the ship. The crew of 90 were very crowded and at times appeared almost to be clambering over each other. The majority of the men seemed of a shorter stature than the people I had been used to seeing ashore. For a moment my youthful brain pondered whether, perhaps, one could fit more sailors on board if they were of smaller proportions. I did come to know, however, that on many a sea voyage one might expect to lose several sailors to disease or misadventure. Captain Salisbury later told me that many other ship's captains who did not follow his practice of stocking sauerkraut as a precaution against scurvy could easily lose as many as two-thirds or more of the crew to this dread disease. He did not expect this to happen to us, he confided, but said that he had had to take a somewhat larger crew than other ships of similar size would have done, because we could expect to face much hardship and deprivation and even potential loss of life on our voyage.

I had heard many a nautical tale at the inn from the sea-farers who would stay a day or two on the way to rejoin their

families or as they awaited their ship's departure heading back
to sea. When I first met Captain Salisbury, in my childish mind
I had expected his ship to be the size of the new palace given to
the Duke of Marlborough after his English and Austrian troops,
despite having been outnumbered, had defeated the French and
the Bavarians at the Battle of Blenheim. Naturally I had never
actually seen this new palace, as Oxford lay a goodly distance
from our inn, but I had heard stories about it from the way-
farers who lodged with us. I did really expect the ship to be of
fantastic proportions, with thousands of exotic-looking sailors
from all parts of the world manning it. In reality, the *Vigour* was
no more than about ten times the size of the White Horse Inn.
I admit I was a wee bit disappointed, but was soon too busy to
notice the size of our floating vessel.

My main duty at first was waiting on Captain Salisbury
and first officer, Samuel Sullivan; the quartermaster, Andrew
Spikes; the boatswain, Ebenezer Swanson; the gunner, John
Hilbert; and the surgeon, Adelbert Loyster. Though still young
in years and with little formal education, I see now that I must
have been rather more quick-witted than most boys my age. I
looked forward to a great future under the tutelage of my kindly
and intelligent mentor.

I soon came to see that the men were busy day and night
with their assigned duties. I could not understand the stories of
mistreatment I had sometimes heard at the inn when sailors com-
plained bitterly of their ill-use at the hands of former masters,
captains and officers — all the more difficult, then, to understand when the common men were the ones doing all the work.
Could their superiors have sailed or lived aboard these vessels

for even five minutes at a time without the constant cooking, cleaning and caulking, what to speak of the maintenance of the ropes, sails, decks and cannons?

At dawn, the first watch of the day came on duty. After they breakfasted on salted sardines, dry biscuits and wine, two olive-skinned crew members set about swabbing the decks with mops and buckets of sea water. The captain and his five officers fared better with their fresh eggs and cream, root vegetables, fruit cordials, wines and sherries along with compotes of dried fruits like raisins, prunes, peaches and apricots, which I was sent to fetch and prepare from the captain-and-gentlemen's pantry, as well as a few delicacies I had never seen before — truffles from France and Spanish olives.

Lookouts took their places in the rigging and at the bow of the ship. The sails were regularly trimmed to take full advantage of the prevailing winds. The six 12-pounder cannons and the 14 eight-pounders were cleaned and checked. Ropes were examined for wear and tear, and the boatswain saw to it that rips in the canvas sails were stitched and repaired immediately.

On one occasion, Captain Salisbury allowed me to take the helm, though very much under the watchful eye of the first officer; I found he jealously guarded this duty as his own whenever we were in port or in proximity to land. Well out to sea as we were, though, I am sure I could have done us little harm even if a sudden wind or swell of sea had tried to take command of the vessel and had thereby made it difficult to hold to our assigned course.

At some point in our voyage I was expected to start training to become a midshipman. We were at sea for three days, while the ship bore on her course. The *Vigour* had steady winds, and the crew proved to be able seamen who took orders with deference to their captain and fellow officers.

The only exception was Ishmael Kratz, a small, swarthy sailor with slightly protruding yellow teeth and an almost nonexistent chin, nearing three score years of age. His physical appearance and demeanour made him seem vaguely ratlike. His evil appearance called to mind the memory of some of the unkempt, disruptive lodgers who had occasionally worn out their welcomes at the White Horse Inn and had had to be hauled off in the wee hours of the morning after a night of drunken revelry.

My brother Ned and I had had to take over from my father the task of dragging these louts outside the public house, to be claimed by their wives in the morning, leading numerous snotty-nosed urchins in tow. This was a task made more difficult if they were roaring drunk and made easier if they had begun to fall asleep from overindulgence. After numerous confrontations, we had learned to observe them in order to gauge the best time to haul them off.

Aboard ship I was kept busy waiting on the captain's table, delivering messages to the carpenter and the various officers, and generally helping wherever I was needed. I was becoming more aware of Kratz's aberrant and disruptive behaviour, and recalled this crewman's disparaging remarks towards the captain and other crew members. His mercurial personality more and more vacillated between maniacal rantings and hysterical laughter resounding throughout the ship.

At times it even appeared to me as if Kratz was trying to

fuel mutiny by hinting or declaring that the captain meant to leave some of the crew marooned on Blackbeard's Island for lack of space to accommodate both the expected vast treasure and all of the men on their return voyage to England.

Kratz was a rumour-monger of the lowest degree. While swabbing decks outside the main cabin, he claimed, he had over-heard a conversation between Captain Salisbury and his officers. He said a disagreement had arisen and a heated dispute ensued amongst them. Kratz had said that the officers had to draw straws, since one of them would have to be left behind too.

The rumour spread as a wildfire would, implying that his superiors were planning to maroon some of the able-bodied seamen whose services would no longer be required, since (as Kratz imputed) they served no purpose in this imagined scheme other than to occupy space and eat his good provisions after the ship's departure from Blackbeard's Island.

Though such behaviour would have run completely counter to the good Captain Salisbury's obvious concern for the health and welfare of all the sailors aboard ship, I do not doubt that at least a few of the more credulous souls did appear to have taken Kratz's poisonous rumour-mongering at face value. The Captain, however, seemed by turns unaware and unconcerned. I entered his cabin once to bring him his breakfast. As I served him, I mentioned the rumours I had heard.

"Don't believe all the stories you may hear aboard a ship, lad," he said. "These are good men. They're not perfect, by any means, but they are all good sailors, and trustworthy. You may be sure that I wouldn't sail with a crew I could not trust."

I looked at an entry he had made in the log:

"We have been at sea for two days. The morale of the men is high. I made sure that among the sailors I chose for this journey was one who could play the fiddle and another whose instrument was a concertina. Music will keep the men's spirits up, since the harsh life at sea and the daily routine of shipboard duties can take a toll on their well-being, both mental and physical. Certainly, physical exercise and lively music will be very beneficial to the ship's morale."

He was indeed a good man, our Captain Salisbury, and I loved him the more when I saw the notation of this minor evidence, confirming once again, if such confirmation were needed, his obvious and sincere concern for his crew.

2.   Simon Crudgely's tale

AFTER THREE WEEKS AT SEA, we sailed into the Portuguese port of Lisbon — a welcome port of call for all of us. The historic rivalries among Dutch, Portuguese, French and English trading companies for control of the lucrative Atlantic slave trade from Africa to trans-shipment points in Curaçao and Jamaica had settled down for the time being. Although Spain was still paying with stolen Peruvian silver for slaves landed at Veracruz and Cartagena, English captains out of Bristol were now purchasing their human cargo from Portuguese colonies in Africa and shipping them, packed up to 450 or 500 at a time, in the holds of slaving ships bound for the Caribbean.

The slave trade was repugnant to all of us aboard the *Vigour*, and no less so to Captain Salisbury. The fact that war with the French had ended for a time and peaceful commercial relations were now possible with countries that had once been our enemies (and might well be so again in future) meant that we faced no particular danger in putting in at a Portuguese port. We would be assured of getting quality goods at a mutually agreed price without being concerned about having to pay smugglers demanding a high price for items that the government harbour authorities might in less peaceful times have judged to be contraband.

In one incident, our ship's quartermaster went ashore and became very intoxicated at a nearby drinking establishment — *O Touro e Laranjeira*. I believe it was to celebrate his sea legs having been planted firmly on *terra firma* again after our most recent sea voyage. He then continued his rounds on an all-night drinking binge, having frequented what seemed to be every other watering hole in this medieval city. Fortunately, he did eventually find his way back to the ship and was able to restore himself to sobriety in time to supervise the lading of our vessel for our next leg of our journey.

Captain Salisbury had made the stopover in the principal harbour of this world-renowned seafaring nation in order to restock our ship with much-needed provisions and water. The quartermaster sported a soiled, water-soaked rag wrapped around his forehead whenever he felt the full effects of his rum and Madeira from the previous day and night. It was all a blur to him. At Lisbon, the *Vigour* had taken on extra supplies for the voyage, including six barrels each of oranges, lemons and limes, which were rolled into the stores cabins. Although we had commonly used lemon juice in combination with sand as a cleanser, and the lemon juice by itself to polish the ship's brass, I now learned of a new use for lemons — indeed, for citrus fruits generally. Our ship's surgeon Dr. Loyster had read John Woodall's treatise, *The Surgeon's Mate;* ours was to be among one of the first voyages to benefit from Woodall's sage advice:

"The juyce of lemmons is a precious medicine and well tried; being sound and good. Let it have the chief place, for it will deserve it. The use whereof is: It is to be taken each morning two or three teaspoonfuls, and fast after it two hours. Some chirurgeons also give of the juyce daily to the men in health as preservative."

While the other officers keenly observed the fine Portuguese Madeira sherry being brought on board by the barrel-full for the personal use of the captain and officers, the good Captain Salisbury, as always, exhibited a genuine concern for the health of his men and personally saw to the stowing of the citrus fruit. He had set an example on a few previous voyages of daily drinking sweetened lime juice with his officers on deck in full sight of his crewmen, who followed his example, though some grumbled, that they would rather have had a double daily ration of rum instead. British sailors eventually came to be called "limeys" after other ships began to adopt Salisbury's healthful practice.

Even today I sadden to think that not all sea captains, despite the certain knowledge of lemons and limes as both a curative and a preventative of scurvy, have yet to adopt this simple measure. The failure to stock limes has cost the lives of thousands of sailors who have unnecessarily died a painful death from a readily preventable disease.

Even cabbage, pickled as *sauerkraut*, has benefit against the scurvy, as many an old sailor will tell you. As I write this account, a Scottish surgeon, James Lind, has recently published his report of having tested different remedies for the scurvy. He had made the initial mistake, however, of thinking that it was the vinegar, rather than the cabbage, in the *sauerkraut* which confers the benefit. The sailors to whom he gave vinegar did not recover, however, but those to whom he gave two oranges and a lemon every day regained their health within a week. Thus it was proved, beyond a shadow of a doubt, that the restorative powers of these most excellent tropical and exotic fruits were scientifically sound.

Truly our new Age of Enlightenment is bearing good fruit, if I may be pardoned a pun, through Dr. Lind's confirming his findings by sound application of the scientific method, with rigorous testing of various initial possibilities enabling him to draw the correct conclusion by analyzing the results, whether harmless but of no effect or beneficial and effective, of each experiment.

Two days out of Lisbon, I was by the ship's rail, queasy and somewhat ill from rough seas, and wishing for the moment that I did not have to be aboard a storm-tossed ship but could fly, like the numerous gulls that thronged wherever one of the galley helpers was tossing buckets of fish guts overboard. It was then that I spotted a small, crude raft of timbers lashed together with lengths of rope. The whole spanned no more than the area of two pub doors, and the tiny raft seemed certain soon to come apart from the impact of the high waves besetting it. Looking more closely, I saw that the craft was inhabited by a lone occupant whose wild, beseeching eyes met mine as he waved both arms furiously to attract my attention.

I immediately informed Captain Salisbury. Commending me for my sharp lookout, despite my protestation that it was the merest chance that I had even been by the rail, he swiftly ordered a boat put out to help rescue the imperilled seaman. Though the waters were still far from smooth, the expert sailors ably manned the boat and rowed towards the raft while carefully tacking at an angle to the most direct route, to ensure that the waves would not overcome them. They then tacked back, reached the raft and rescued its occupant, whom they quickly brought aboard the *Vigour*.

I was most surprised to learn that the rescued raftsman was a young man not yet 20, named Simon Crudgely. He had tufts of sandy-brown hair bobbing on his head, along with piercing green eyes, a short turned-up nose and ruddy cheeks. Though much younger than my crewmates, he possessed a surprisingly mature and independent spirit. Only the carpenter's apprentice and I were younger than he was, and naturally we admired his tenacious ability to survive alone at sea.

Simon revealed to us that he had put to sea as a baker and cook, but his ship had sunk near the Azores. He had heard the call to board the lifeboats, but having been for the moment trapped in the galley by fallen debris which blocked his exit, he had been unable to get to one of the boats before their departure. Eventually clearing the blockage away from the door and escaping from the galley, he had managed to swim to a tiny offshore island. He did not know what had become of the remaining ship's crew, but he cherished the faint hope that they had been saved.

Unfortunately for him, the island was uninhabited, and he had then feared he might never be rescued. From bits of ship's wreckage, therefore, he had fashioned together his rough raft and put out again to sea, hoping to sail to one of the nearby inhabited islands in the same Azores archipelago. He had skilfully assembled a relatively seaworthy raft; however, he was no sailor or navigator, and the wind and currents had pushed his tiny, makeshift craft further out to the open sea, instead of towards an island. That was how we had come upon him so far from any nearby land.

The Captain and the crew and I were uniformly astonished at his survival and at his indomitable spirit. Although he was at least six years older than I, his admirable qualities made me readily look up to him; indeed, we soon became fast friends, as he shared with me the story of his childhood, his philosophy of life and his seafaring experiences.

We would meet on deck in the evenings when our chores were done, as Simon was taken on a cook's helper and baker on our ship. We would discuss various questions and experiences which had puzzled us both in our search for truth and justice in this Age of Enlightenment. Simon wasn't highly educated, but he was very intelligent and observant of life and his fellow human beings in the relatively brief time he had lived in the world of immoral, abnormal, harsh and wicked wealthy men.

The riches of lords and kings, Simon began, could scarce compare with true and virtuous happiness. Most times, bitter people gain wealth and fame either through accident of birth or through cunning, violence and deceit. Possession of unearned and unmerited wealth serves to poison the soul and mind, since it replaces morality and human values like kindness, whilst enslaving "lesser" honest and genuine people to do the wealthy people's dirty work both literally and figuratively.

I readily agreed that to gain such wealth, one must sell one's soul to the devil. Gold never makes one truly happy, however, unless that wealth is used to help those less fortunate and deserving. Herein is to be found the secret to happiness, which really isn't all that much of a secret at all. The sages of the ages have known this from time immemorial. Sharing one's success in deeds of sincerest generosity brings far more real, genuine happiness than mere acquisitiveness and accumulation of fortune ever could.

Indeed, during frequent musings on life I have sometimes wondered why anybody, aside from the dear God in heaven, should expect to be addressed as "Lord." In my youth I would speak as the social order demanded, but now I find such a mode of address arrogant, grating, presumptuous and a sop to the vanity of the conceited. The behaviour of these individuals has always, for the most part, been so far from God-like, anyway, so as to be in league with the devil, to be perfectly accurate and honest.

Simon then related his most curious tale of wantonness, the fuller details of which he had only recently learned of himself. His mother Edwina had been happy as a milkmaid on the outskirts of Bristol, but her youthful beauty had attracted the unwelcome attentions of Lord Dunston, who still held the attitude that might was right. Indeed, he even took the position that as the right of *seigneury* overrode the rights of all except the divine right of kings, he could wantonly ignore the rights of others, certainly those of his tenants or others in his employ. That good woman had taken on a new life since fleeing a forced carnal encounter with her craven, exploiting employer — a union that occurred during the time she had been employed in his household.

Arriving in her new village, Edwina had told people the tale that her husband had been lost at sea while serving as a mariner in the Caribbean. Factually, she did want to start a new life, being already with child at the time, though she told no one. Simon had never been told the truth of his origins. His beloved mother wanted to spare him from this unseemly side of her life, though her embarrassment had obviously not been her fault, and she desperately wanted to hide the story of her past life in this new village. Edwina wished to make a new start for the baby she was carrying — to protect both her own future and that of her unborn child.

As the year began, the young lass of seventeen also forged a new identity, initially taking as her own the surname of the parson of her village church who had passed away a decade ago. He had been a kindly, elderly gentleman. As she was fond of this individual from her past and greatly respected him, she took his name, wishing that her life and that of her unborn child would be as blessed as the fine parson's had been. She had observed in her brief life that people in their old age, and sometimes younger, wear their personality and traits on their face, reflecting the kind of life they have led in the world and what deeds they have committed. The parson's face had been imbued with the soft lines of kindness, purity and good humour. Edwina heartily wished to follow in his footsteps.

She soon obtained work in the new village bakery, having learned much of the art of bread- and pastry-making whilst working in the kitchen of his lordship's manor, where she had originally entered service at the age of 12. Albert Crudgely, owner of the baker's shop and a jolly, kind-hearted soul of about 30, had hired Edwina on the spot when she came to inquire as to the possibility of employment. He had an ample, rotund form that reflected his love of fine pastries — a love, nevertheless, which was soon exceeded by his love for Simon's mother.

Albert had been smitten from the time he first set eyes upon the pretty lass as she unlatched the door to the bakery. Often, between batches of hot cross buns and his famous Cornish pasties, Albert had glanced at her admiringly as she served the customers with fresh-faced honesty and grace and a kindness that could never be feigned. Edwina, too, had felt an attraction to this kind, considerate and loving person. She had married Crudgely a scant month later, after he proposed to her — kneeling before her in his floury baker's smock, of course.

Young Simon was born nearly nine months after the marriage of his happy and adoring parents. Undoubtedly wanting to prolong his enjoyment of the pastries his mother was now consuming, baby Simon overstayed his tenancy in her womb and made more plausible a conception date that was at least a month after the true event. His baker father never knew the truth of the matter, and loved Simon more than anyone else in the world except for Edwina herself, and certainly more than Lord Dunston ever would — or was capable of doing. Crudgely was delighted at the thought of having fathered a baby boy.

Simon's mother and her kind-hearted baker husband were an excellent match — the very picture of the domestic bliss that reigned supreme in their modest yet happy household. Their cups ran over with goodness, mutual kindness and contentment.

In his manor house in a neighbouring county, the obesely beset Dunston grew ever more corpulent and distended as he feasted on the villagers' food, which they had grown by the sweat of their brows, rising early in the morning and tilling fields to the point of utter exhaustion, stopping only briefly for a hurried noon meal in the shade of a large elm. His lordship literally rolled out of bed at least seven hours after his workers, to be wined and dined at his leisure.

Tenants on his estate, on the other hand, often came close to starving, due to the high rents he assessed. He also demanded onerous taxes on behalf of the Crown, but deviously held back the lion's share for himself. These forms of abuse have been the bane of the common man since the dawn of civilization.

It was no exaggeration to say that by thus confiscating much of his tenants' means of subsistence, Lord Dunston was taking the food from the tenant children's mouths, yet his cruelty towards them scarcely troubled his conscience. He was sorely lacking in heart and mind; like many of those among his class, he truly lacked a moral compass. In fact, he was one of those for whom there were seemingly no calibrations on their instruments at all. Their superficial and mindless lifestyle and infantile state of mind were and are to this day perpetrated for the sake of the continuance of their social class.

He had misspent his youth in idle pursuits like galloping around the countryside on horseback, chasing small, defence-less foxes with hounds. The lives of their overburdened mounts were needlessly risked during these pointless pursuits and ritual-ized murders of animals he had no intent to eat. The rich and stupid — or, shall we say, those that were and are soft in the head and weak in the flesh — lack rhyme, reason or purpose on earth. Indeed, the world would have been a happier, better place without them befouling it. Many a fine mind must also have been wasted that could have helped humanity in its betterment, which would have been a true sign of class and good upbringing.

My impression of the man, as I heard of him from Simon, soured still more when he related how Dunston was not merely the "owner" of two house-servants, an arrangement tolerated by the law though much campaigned against by abolitionists, but a major portion of his income represented the profits of his financing of vessels trading in sugar, rum and human slaves. Had he been a man of ordinary means, the character reflected in his face might have been totally different and pleasing to the mind and soul even at his age in life.

Kindness and gentleness, when tempered with compassion, produces a purity of spirit and mind which is unmatched by any possession or wealth, a purity which in turn produces true and eternal happiness and which puts the mind at ease that one is doing what was intended in the normal scheme of things and the world. Goodness radiates from such a soul through one's countenance, eyes and pleasing personality. They are all windows of the soul; God in heaven intended it so. Then and only then are man and woman truly happy. One cannot buy this at a village market or as the most costly item in a merchant's emporium. It must be earned from doing good deeds in life and in the service of one's fellow man and woman over a lifetime.

Meantime, however, Simon grew to look more and more like the absentee lord, taking on some of Lord Dunston's facial characteristics as he matured.

Master Simon did not find out about his origins in life until several years after an incident that had occurred when he was a freckle-faced lad of fourteen. His lordship, Sir Dunston, had long since forgotten Simon's mother, as he had similarly put out of his lecherous head the names of many other virtuous girls he had deflowered. Travelling to London, he had stopped in Edwina's and Simon's new village for the night after the wheels of his coach had become lodged in the ruts of a muddy road not a quarter mile away.

The generously girthed lord, by then nearing twenty-five stone, came huffing and puffing, his cheeks flushed, into the main square of town, having been forced to walk to the village. This rare exertion made Lord Dunston ravenously hungry and winded after walking this short distance. Spying the bakery shingle outside the establishment of Simon Crudgely's father, his lordship sought sustenance in this storefront on Kings Road adjacent to the *Crown and Rose* public house. His prominent proboscis led him into these savoury surroundings, shall we say, and the rest of his amply sized lordship naturally followed suit, almost floating into the building. The enticing smell was simply too much for the large-bottomed lordship to resist.

Albert Crudgely had been instructing Simon about the finer points of making Cornish pasties. He cherished the hope that one day the lad would also become a baker, thus helping to provide for his father and mother in their old age and enabling the already respectable and relatively prosperous business to remain in the family for the next generation.

Dunston, on first spying the young lad busy at his trade, was startled beyond measure at seeing his own image reflected in

Simon's face. The similarity was all the more acutely unnerving because the dining room of his grand manorial home featured a baroquely framed formal oil painting of Dunston himself that had been commissioned by the previous Lord Dunston when the family scion was only ten. He had gazed at that painting almost every day of his subsequent life. Thus, although he was now vastly more corpulent, he still maintained a perfect mental image of himself at ten, and he now compared this inner picture with the face of the boy he observed rolling out pastries, spooning on filling, folding over edges and crimping to seal them tightly.

In his present physical state, of course, Dunston had lost any former physical attractiveness he might have had, as well as whatever mental prowess he had once exhibited. At 68, his physical attributes and countenance had been much distorted by a licentious lifestyle and gluttonous ways. Endless days of mindless passion — sometimes hunting foxes on the moors, sometimes demanding cruel rents and sometimes witnessing a bailiff's taking possession of lands and homes from tenant farmers when the crop had been poor — punctuated by bouts of painful gout and endless nights of drunken revelry had conspired with his evil career as a merciless slave trader and financier to take their toll on him physically and mentally. They registered on his pale, flaky and pock-marked skin. His life of debauchery and deceit could almost be read in his depraved, dishevelled and generally unwholesome appearance.

Dunston, still dumbfounded, continued his close study of young Simon's resemblance to himself. The 'nobleman' was visibly taken aback by his realization, but attempted to recover his composure and to dismiss from his undisciplined mind this finding most unpleasant to himself. From his overbearing father he had learned in childhood to ignore whatever he did not wish to acknowledge.

Indeed, Dunston's father had laid stress on the maxim that children were to be seen but not heard. Such conventional claptrap had been based on his relentlessly selfish and tradition-bound society, which ruled their world in a way that stifled demonstrations of morality, family affection or anything that resembled normalcy. Their progeny only existed for the purpose of perpetuating the *status quo* and their outdated and mentally weak social class and oppressive structure.

For once in his life, he knew neither what to do and say nor how to escape this new situation in which he inopportunely found himself. Simon's visage reminded the old aristocrat of his youthful innocence and made him realize his great remove from that pure state of youth. This was the first time in his life that he'd felt even a twinge of any sort of guilt and remorse for his despicable, self-indulgent and wasted life — a hitherto pointless existence of unmitigated idleness and licentiousness.

Then Simon's mother came forward to the sales counter from the inner recesses of the bakery to check on her son's progress on muffin and bread orders for the *Crown and Rose*. Now quite certain of his relationship to the boy, he became utterly unglued by the untimely appearance of his former maid, and his mind flashed back to their last encounter.

"What's this now?" he said, looking her full in the face and blurting out the words uncontrollably, with an even more astonished look on his face.

Simon's mother recoiled in greater dread, even horror,

than his, feeling instant revulsion at the sight of this cruel and corpulent brute who now dared stand before her after what he had done to her. She fainted on the spot.

Albert came quickly to her rescue. After her husband administered some spirits of ammonia, Edwina gave out a loud gasp and quickly regained consciousness. "Are you all right then, luv'?" he asked worriedly, her head cradled in his arms while he was bent over her body on the wooden floor.

"I'll be as right as rain if I can rest a little," she replied with a faint voice. "I'll just lie here for a moment or two until I feel better, Albert."

"What made you faint, luv'?" he questioned, with great concern in his voice. "Are you keeping back a little secret from me, p'rhaps?"

"Albert, you need not worry. Mayhap you'd be the one fainting, not me, if you knew the full of it," she answered sweetly. "P'rhaps it was that extra pasty I et today," she explained, trying to divert his attention.

Much to her relief, his lordship — preceded, naturally, by his flaring snout and followed, of course, by his still more ample *derrière* — had fled the bakery as quickly as the storied Merlin of King Arthur's day might have disappeared amidst a colourful cloud of smoke. The bell over the door was still ringing after the brute had hastily made good his retreat. She needed no ghosts from the past to haunt her at this time in her life — nor at any other time either. Simon had a loving father and devoted mother now. This is the way she wished it to remain.

Lord Dunston scattered into the streets like the dirty, rat-like being that he was. He was last seen tottering out the village, rounding the corner and down the main cobblestoned road, breathing rapidly, sweating profusely and clutching his tricorn hat.

His short brown periwig had been snatched off his head by a sharp gust, then flew about in the breeze until it landed backwards on a shire horse's head. The gelding had been waiting for his master patiently as the brewer rolled out the barrels in front of the *Crown and Rose*. His lordship was quite bareheaded and bald as he made a bee-line through the main street, jiggling and bouncing up and down and leaving the village in the dust.

Lord Dunston was never again seen by anyone in that county. Some say he was robbed and shot by a highwayman who relieved him of both his lecherous, directionless life and his heavy purse. Others suggest he was so distraught and shocked that he mounted a horse backwards and bounced out of town facing its rear whilst villagers broke into peals of laughter.

But while people still do relate these stories, the simple truth was that the innkeeper had simply located a team of oxen, and they had been dispatched to the place where Dunston's coach had become stuck in the mud. The most likely explanation is the innkeeper's tale — that they freed the coach from the mud which had threatened to swallow up the wheels, and the coach continued to its destination or returned to his manor house.

As people debated which of the stories might be true, they would erupt in laughter anew on recalling how they had bid him farewell from their village by mockingly bowing and curtseying in the direction of his disappearing lordship. Dunston's sudden departure from this part of England had been certainly neither aristocratic nor genteel, and villagers felt some gratitude at the amusement he had provided them — one of the best japes they had experienced that year or, perhaps, for the last two years.

Not for many years did her husband learn the reason she had fainted that day in the bakery, nor did Edwina tell Simon himself until after his eighteenth birthday, as she was determined to save her family from experiencing unnecessary turmoil. In any case, the notoriety would not have been of her doing, but society has an unreasonable way of punishing the poor and innocent while allowing the rich and guilty to get off scot-free. With threats based on their social standing and social class, they can bully their way out of any situation. It is hypocritical, dishonest, unfair and undeserved, but it is the way of the world, though wholly unfair to all good, upstanding people. After he became an adult, Simon's mother told him the truth of his conception, as well as of the trials and tribulations his mother had had to endure in her lifetime at the hands of this swine of a lord.

I commiserated with Simon over his mother's suffering at the hands of this useless, immoral, abnormal aristocrat, but reminded him that despite this, his childhood had been happy and that he had a family that loved him. Also, now he had a useful trade as a baker.

That skill was now in demand, evidently, for we soon heard Mr. McCaury's voice demanding to know where he had gotten to. Standing over Simon and shaking his index finger at him, the coxswain interrupted our conversation and told us to get busy promptly. Evidently his having been rescued at sea offered him no exemption from shipboard work.

"Simon, lad, I've been looking for ya, and you too, Master Christopher! Where 'ave you been? You've been as scarce as 'ens' teeth. Fetch me four buckets of good potatoes to the galley and set to peeling them. No dillydallying, mind you, or you'll get a sound boxing of your ears too, you will."

We needed no second prompting, and did as we were told. In the galley we saw the ship's cook flourishing a bandaged hand; he had injured himself in cutting or chopping, so we had been pressed into food preparation tasks. The cook, though obviously unable for now to continue his duties, could still direct us in their correct execution.

3. A ghost ship appears

AFTER RESCUING SIMON from near-certain jaws of death, we sailed uneventfully for a few days, yet I noticed that some of the men were already getting restless. Again, perhaps, despite the Captain's sunny optimism, the unfounded gossip of the low scoundrel, Kratz, was beginning to take effect. There was grumbling to be heard. The men's formal education had, for the most part, been cut short at an early stage in the primary grades. Incurious and lacking higher pursuits, they were men who amused themselves below decks in the evenings with drinking, playing cards or dancing jigs to the accompaniment of the ships' fiddler or concertina player. I continued to hope for the best, while beginning to fear the worst.

"Ship ho! Five leagues hence, approaching from starboard on the half sail!" McTavish announced from his perch in the crow's nest. Captain Salisbury approached the mast with a spyglass in his hand, and heard the lookout utter an exclamation in a tone of questioning surprise. "Be it Spanish, then?"

This was promptly followed by another observation from the crow's nest. "There's somethin' not quite right, cap'n, with this 'ere vessel," continued the lookout.

"Correct, Mr. McTavish," said the Captain, as he peered intently through the glass. "The flag appears to be Spanish, all right, but it's flying upside down," he continued. "It seems very suspicious indeed, since no one is visible on deck either."

"We'll approach with caution, Mr. Spikes." The quartermaster changed the *Vigour's* course to bring the two ships broadside. The Captain passed the spyglass to the boatswain.

"The galleon's sails are tattered, in poor repair. Perhaps it's a ghost ship abandoned by her crew," Swanson suggested.

"A trap set by pirates, more likely!" added the boatswain with suspicion. "Maybe they're hiding below decks, planning to attack us unawares!"

"We're totally vulnerable now!" said the first officer. His Scots accent made the word sound something like "woon'rible." We were all surprised to come upon an apparently unmanned ship so far out at sea. Indeed, we used sometimes to sail for days or weeks without encountering another vessel of any kind.

Inwardly, the Captain's mind raced with apprehension at the thought of encountering unknown foes. Without naval support, they would be left entirely to their own devices to beat off a pirate attack — although I supposed they could certainly make use of the ship's guns if needed. He had to think fast.

"Nonsense, man," he said, with some bravado. "What would a ship like this be doing in the middle of the ocean? Clearly, it's a merchant ship, since it does not carry any large guns or cannon." At first he was dismissive, then he conceded the point.

"Maybe the crew died from scurvy, the plague or a tropical fever. The ship may have lost its way in the doldrums, only to have the crew starve, or the ship may have lost its moorings and drifted here." He looked back at Spikes. "It appears to be adrift, and listing to starboard. We must work quickly to salvage what we can and save any survivors, if there be any."

Neil McTavish had quickly clambered down from the crow's nest. "Captain! The decks on the Spanish ship are covered with people! I canna' tell if they'r-r-re sleeping or dead, but they do appear-r-r to be all ages — men, women and childr-r-ren are spr-r-rawl'd about."

Salisbury was equally shocked and startled. "What?" he blurted, taken aback by the gruff Scotsman's observation.

"I don't r-r-rightly know if the victims on ship are dead or alive. It do appear-r-r as if they'r-r-re sleeping. Ther-r-re's no sign of blood or foul play."

After Salisbury determined there was no imminent danger to ourselves, he gave the orders to board the Spanish vessel at once. "We must work fast. There may be lives in the balance!"

The name of the other ship was easily identified. It was the *Santa Teresita*. A crewman threw a grappling hook towards the Spanish ship to draw it closer, so the captain and crew of the *Vigour* could investigate the mystery of what had happened to the unconscious passengers on board. The hook caught midships, around a railing. Four other crew members helped him haul the ship broadside to their own. The ships were also lashed together with hemp ropes, so sailors could readily cross over with medical supplies, water or food if and when the mysterious passengers roused.

Injured and infirm individuals could be easily transferred from ship to ship with minimal difficulty and effort. Leaving his first officer in charge of the *Vigour*, Captain Salisbury was the first to board the mysterious Spanish ship. He climbed over the railings where the ships were bound together. Three of the ordinary seamen, along with the surgeon, the carpenter and the boatswain, followed suit, as did I.

What lay before us was a shocking sight. A swarthy crew in their blue-and-white-striped naval uniforms, about 20 or so, lay alongside several women wearing fashionable and genteel pastel green and lavender outfits. It appeared as if the men had come to their assistance after the women had swooned on the spot. Where they had been felled was a mysterious mauve substance discoloured to yellow at the edges — a powdery residue which I suspected of having been in some part the cause of their present predicament.

Everyone lay on the deck without any outward appearance of bleeding or obvious foul play. They did not appear to have been taken from this world but seemed to be sleeping comfortably, with normal, rhythmic breathing, as was observed by Captain Salisbury.

Another ten or so men, women and children lay similarly unconscious on the wooden deck in the same condition as the others. Salisbury's crew at first approached them cautiously, and were much relieved when they ascertained that the stricken people did not constitute any threat to their life or limb. The felled people on the deck were in no condition to attack or do them any harm. Dr. Loyster, who was summoned by the good Captain, knelt by each of them in turn to examine their vital signs. He placed his ear to every chest, felt every pulse and, with a small looking-glass under each victim's nostrils and mouth, checked carefully to satisfy himself that all of them were breathing. Seeing the surgeon's bold example, the crew approached them, first cautiously, then more confidently when the unconscious people strewn about did not rouse.

The passengers and crew — for the most part, they were found lying on their backs — appeared as if they had been given a powerful sleeping draught, or had been overcome with some overwhelming emotional trauma. Some, however, lay face down, but when the doctor rolled them on their backs to be examined, they seemed surprisingly normal. Far from the pallour that is imparted to those who are departed from this world, they all seemed to have a healthy glow in their cheeks and faces.

Aside from appearing to be sleeping soundly, in all other respects they seemed quite the picture of health. Though breathing with a steady rhythm, they were still unconscious. What had befallen them? This was the obvious mystery to be solved at this time.

They did not rouse after being examined, even after their skin began to redden as they lay exposed to the tropical noonday sun. Very concerned, the Captain told his men to help Doctor Loyster carry them — some inside the forecastle and the rest underneath a large sail stretched out horizontally and tethered with ropes as an improvised awning.

"It looks as if their skin is reacting to the sun," Loyster said. "Put wet cloths soaked in water on their exposed skin, especially their faces. It will soothe them and stop them from burning any further," the doctor continued.

Captain Salisbury promptly commanded two burly seamen to manœuvre one of our casks of fresh water onto the main deck of the *Vigour* and to roll it carefully over planks placed amidships to the *Santa Teresita*. The seas were idyllically calm, and the placid waters minimized the ships' rolling and facilitated the transfer of men, water and medical supplies — sheets, salves and light blankets taken from the stores room. The sea cooperated with them in this time of need and presented a stark contrast to the veritable beehive of activity on the decks of both vessels. Inside the forecastle and under the canvas canopy numerous sailors were attending to the unconscious victims, all now draped in water-soaked white sheets like grave-shrouds.

The Captain found a lady of obvious great wealth, readily discernible from her ornate and fashionable clothing, bejewelled neck and fair complexion — all of which evidenced that she certainly did not work in the hot sun doing manual labour on a plantation or estate. Her fingers were long, white and slender, neatly manicured like a lady of leisure. He checked her pulse, and she appeared to be breathing normally, as the others were. Salisbury immediately summoned the surgeon to come to the aid of this unfortunate lady and to re-examine all of the other people scattered about the deck.

"Dr. Loyster, do they have some contagious disease, perhaps?" Salisbury asked, obviously concerned that his own crew might become infected with the same contagion.

"I can't be sure as yet, captain. I don't have any diagnosis presently. All we can do is to make the patients as comfortable as possible until they all, God willing, regain consciousness. Then they can tell us their story, and this mystery will become more clear," Loyster explained, quite puzzled and dumbfounded with the situation he now found himself in.

"In the meantime, I suggest that we quarantine all these people on their own ship. In case it is a tropical disease, their ship should be isolated from ours and anchored a short distance away from our vessel so they do not infect us — or until, at least, we can determine what their condition is. The sailors who have helped me handle the patients should stay in quarantine with me as well. Also we must check below deck to see if there are any more similarly afflicted people here like this so they can all be treated at the same time. They should all remain here so that we do not risk the spread of any disease to our own people on the *Vigour*."

To all of this the Captain readily acquiesced, and everything was done as the doctor had suggested. The *Santa Teresita* was to be transformed into a temporary floating hospital vessel for as long as necessary until all of the crew and passengers were fit and capable of travel again. Huge sheets of canvas from the ship's stores were strung across the deck to provide more shade for the patients still littering the deck, since the noonday sun would otherwise beat down on them mercilessly in these tropical climes. Captain Salisbury joined them on the *Santa Teresita*, having delegated command of the *Vigour* to the very capable first officer, Mr. Samuel Sullivan.

I was ordered to accompany five other crew members — Mr. Spikes, the quartermaster, along with Messrs. Hilbert, McCaffrey, Ramshott and Totwyssel — to go below deck to seek out and rescue any more sailors or passengers who might be stricken with the same unknown affliction.

Across from the carpenter's quarters below deck, I found the cook of the Spanish ship, collapsed on the floor in his galley. He was lying next to the stove with a black iron ladle still clasped in his hand. He had apparently been serving out bowls of stew from a large kettle when the unknown incident had occurred. I told Mr. Totwyssel about the cook, so that they could carry him on deck.

Returning to the galley kitchen, I observed that the galley stove was still quite hot to the touch and the fire had died back to embers only, so it was clear that whatever calamity had befallen these individuals strewn on deck up above us must have happened at least several hours previously, but not more than a day or so. I knew this because having had to tend many a fire at the White Horse Inn, I had noticed that I could regularly restart a fire from last night's embers with very little effort, as long as they still retained their cheery glow.

I went back on deck and mentioned the still-heated stove to the Captain. He commended me for my "keen and useful observation," elaborating: "It confirms what Mr. Swanson said. He told me he noticed the smell of sulphur when he went below. The surgeon thinks such a smell would not linger about for more than a day. Dr. Loyster conjectured that the chemical smell had something to do with causing the passengers to faint, and that what befell them must have happened very recently too, confirming my initial observation."

Looking dumbfounded, a crewman approached the English captain. "Cap'n Salisbury, come quickly," he said breathlessly. He had just emerged from the bowels of the ship and was now dutifully reporting his findings too.

"What is it, Ramshott?" Salisbury asked tersely. The crewman was evidently having some difficulty in formulating his thoughts.

"What is it, man? Spit it out!" Salisbury reiterated impatiently, almost spitting out his own words in the process through clenched teeth, with his jaws and lips tightening with tension.

"Sir, there is a most strange creature in the officers' quarters," was his reply.

"What on earth are you on talking about, man?" the Captain replied. "Explain yourself!"

"Follow me, sir; it's most urgent!"

As they carefully descended the steep ship's ladder to the lower deck, much shouting erupted. Mr. Totwyssel tried to go up the stairs, but saw Salisbury and Ramshott coming down, and quickly thought better of it. He would not have been able to pass them on the narrow steps, so he instead ran off to the right.

"Cap'n, cap'n! 'e's goin' peck me bloomin' 'ead off, 'e is," the fuzzy-haired blond crewman screamed. "Be off wit' you, you vile creature!"

As he stepped off the bottom rung of the deck ladder, Captain Salisbury was met with the unexpected sight of Mr. Totwyssel being pursued by a huge grey-brown bird with a long neck, such as none of the men had seen or heard tell of before. It was about 8 feet tall and must have weighed close to 10 stone.

"Maybe he likes you," Mr. Bartlesby teased, "or maybe he thinks you're lunch or supper." The ship's carpenter had a bemused look on his face as Mr. Totwyssel ran by a second time, still with the bird in hot pursuit.

"This is no laughing matter," said the captain, angrily.

Salisbury knew full well that this creature was very dangerous and, at the very least, could poke out an eye. The bird pecked at Totwyssel's head with his sharp beak, but luckily only grazed against his skull.

"We have to capture the bird before he injures someone," the captain said to the astonished men by his side. Their eyes were bulging and mouths agape, never having seen such a strange-looking creature in all their days. Salisbury, on the other hand, had observed an illustration of just such a specimen in a Dutch naturalist's book dealing with the flora and fauna of South Africa.

"Be careful to always keep the bird in front of you, and you will be less in danger of it attacking you with its beak or claws." Salisbury warned. "The claws are razor-sharp, and a kick can open up a man's belly."

As the bird continued to chase Totwyssel, he made good his escape into the officers' dining quarters. There he hid under the dark wooden dining table, while the ostrich bobbed to and fro, occasionally lunging at the terrorized crewman with its huge beak.

Captain Salisbury had Mr. Bartlesby fetch two large planks. When the carpenter returned with the boards, Salisbury motioned for the still frightened Totwyssel to run upstairs. He then directed Ramshott and Swanson to hold one quarter-sawn board between them, while he and Bartlesby held another. Standing on either side of the ostrich, they managed to corral the squawking bird and, with nudges from the planks, directed it back into its cage. The bird continued to protest its renewed confinement with loud shrieks and much pecking aimed at the necks and shoulders of its captors. At that point Salisbury took a large black cloth sack, which had been hanging from a hook on the wall, and threw it over the cage; it seemed to calm the ostrich almost immediately.

After all the excitement died down, the sailors gathered up several smaller feathers and a very large one the bird had lost during her recapture.

Salisbury thought that once they returned to England he might have a milliner fashion them into a hat for his wife; it would make a pretty adornment for her, and for him would serve to commemorate their eventful experience.

They later found out, upon inquiry of the captain and officers of the *Santa Teresita*, that their ship was just returning from Melilla, a Spanish town on the Barbary Coast, and had brought the bird on board as a present for the King of Spain, who had been the financier of their voyage. King Felipe V had exotic zoos, first established by the cruel King Felipe II, in Aranjuez and "Casa de Campo" in Madrid, and the *Santa Teresita* had been bound for Seville and Córdoba to deliver its cargo and royal gift.

What probably had happened, thought Salisbury, was that the Spanish crew member who last had fed the ostrich had carelessly left its cage unlocked. Later that day, after all the crew had fallen unconscious and no one had returned to feed her — it appeared as if there were three large eggs the size of cannonballs in her straw nest — she had left her cage and had naturally begun to roam the space below deck in search of food and water. Thus the mystery of the *Santa Teresita* and the ostrich had been partially solved.

4. The Spanish passengers awaken

SOON THE STRICKEN PASSENGERS on the hospital ship began to rouse from their prolonged and mysterious ailment. They groaned, not knowing where they were and what had transpired in the previous days. Men, women, and children alike began moving restlessly and speaking incoherently, a likely side-effect of their condition. With many people talking at once in a multiplicity of dialects, it sounded, I imagined, like the noise that might have been made by the people surrounding the Tower of Babel.

A plump Spanish lady, her arms, legs and face bright red with smallish yellow spots, was being transported to the make-shift hospital ward of the ship when she regained consciousness. Two burly sailors were carrying her, lashed to a 16-inch plank. She looked aghast at her almost tomato-red hands and arms. When the sailors untied her from the plank and put her down on a straw cushion, she caught a glimpse of her reflection in a broken looking-glass and began to scream hysterically as she touched her equally red face with the tips of her delicate fingers. Having seen her normally fair countenance in such a state of disarray, she swooned on the spot.

Meanwhile, one of the Spanish gentlemen had also roused, his head rising slightly from the ship's deck and shifting back and forth slowly. He moaned a little. Then, startled at being surrounded by strangers aboard his ship, his eyelids flickered and opened wide. He was obviously taken aback by what he felt to be unwarranted and unwanted attention.

"*¿Quién es usted? ¿Qué es el significado . . . ? ¿Qué ha pasado aquí?*"

"*No me dolió, ni cualquiera de mis pasajeros, yo mendigo de usted, por favor,*" he continued more slowly, in the Castilian accent of an educated gentleman.

The captain was taken aback. "What is he saying? Does anyone speak Spanish here?" he inquired. "Come to the aid of this man! He may be injured. We need to determine what has transpired, so the infirm passengers can be treated immediately and accordingly."

Another of the Spanish passengers — obviously a rather well-heeled person, a gentleman of means, as demonstrated by his fine attire, and whose goateed face resembled that of a conquistador from the days of yore — had by now roused from his enforced sleep.

Introducing himself as the ship's surgeon for the *Santa Teresita*, he stepped forward hesitatingly, almost mincingly, still feeling the dizzying after-effects of his mysterious condition.

"I can help, Señor Capitán," he said. "Doctor Antonio Martinez da Silva, at your service."

He explained, in English, that he had sailed with a Spanish merchant fleet as a doctor on board and had been captured by the British in a naval skirmish near the mouth of the Amazon. The swarthy fellow had proven his usefulness to his English captors, after their own surgeon had died from dysentery. The Spaniard had also nursed the injured British captain back to health — using particular herbs, potions and poultices — when an Amazonian native, angered at interlopers despoiling the sacred lands of their forefathers, had wounded the Englishman by casting a spear in his left shoulder.

Martinez da Silva had been hired on the spot by the English privateer to serve as a ship's doctor and as an invaluable interpreter for negotiations between Spanish and Portuguese merchant traders, privateers and pirates who dealt in ill-gotten goods — slaves, stolen treasures, jewellery, gold plate, religious artefacts and gold bullion. Returning eventually to his homeland, he continued his study of English at the university in Córdoba and, two years later, again set sail as ship's doctor on the *Santa Teresita*.

The captain addressed Martinez. "What was this man saying? Is he injured?"

"He seems a little confused, and was just pleading with you not to harm his passengers. This is the Captain of our ship, Capitán Juan Alvarez di Carlos."

Captain Salisbury acknowledged him with a slight nod of his head and helped the man to sit upright. At that point a great moan issued from a Spanish lady who had been carried to a cushion on the deck. Immediately, the Spanish doctor turned his attention to her.

"Señorita, are you injured?" asked the Spaniard in his native language, with great concern in his voice, as the young noblewoman pulled herself up slowly to a sitting position.

"No," replied the raven-tressed young lady, weakly.

"What happened to you and the other people on the ship? What caused you and the others to fall into this unconscious state?"

Doctor Martinez translated the woman's story. She related to him such events as she could recall, up to the time she had lost consciousness. "Señor Valdez, one of the crew members, was an alchemist or apothecary," he told the Captain. "He had brought chemicals, potions, and large glass bottles on board, saying that he planned to perform scientific experiments to test flora or fauna that might prove to be of economic value to the king's coffers or yield scientific data."

After further questioning of the young señorita, the Captain learned that the apothecary had not instructed the crew on how to properly secure his equipment and potions to the wall of his cabin, since he had forgotten to order metal bracing for his makeshift ship's laboratory. It was virtually impossible to safely store his potentially dangerous chemicals. He had instead attached them to his walls with braided sisal rope shelves in anticipation of inclement weather and rocky ship movements.

The señorita had helped the apothecary stock his shelves with her servants and listened intently to his descriptions of his researches into these New World products. She soon took quite an interest in his experiments and discoveries herself.

Though her grandfather had lost many a speculated peso in the bursting of the South Sea Bubble some forty years previously, her father still looked for business opportunities, specifically for profits to be made through trading small quantities of finished goods for gold and jewellery.

As ill luck would have it, the *Santa Teresita* had been caught in a heavy storm near the Azores, far more severe than anything the apothecary had ever anticipated, during which the unsecured bottles were tossed all over the alchemist's cabin. The señorita had been visiting the apothecary at this time as the storm arose. Some of the spilled chemicals mixed to form a smoky concoction which engulfed the whole ship and everyone on board, who had collapsed like marionettes in its oncoming path.

"I can remember my father fainting helplessly to the deck in an unconscious stupor," she continued. "As I ran to his aid from the apothecary's lab, I must have myself become overcome from the smoke. That is the last thing I can recall until I regained my consciousness just now." Through Doctor Martinez, our kindly Captain thanked her for her explanation and inquired about the present whereabouts of the apothecary Valdez. Salisbury would send men below deck to find out the fate of the missing chemist.

This description of events relieved our Captain's mind in another way as well. "Surely this means there is no contagion aboard, and no need for quarantining their vessel. Isn't that right?" he asked Doctor Loyster.

The doctor quickly confirmed the Captain's assumption, and Salisbury countermanded his previous order to separate the two ships.

"Is everyone alive?" another young Spanish lady inquired, her brow furrowed deeply, as she slowly moved to stand up too.

"My father, my father, where is he now? *¡Mi padre! ¡Mi padre!*" she said, suddenly conscious of his absence. "I fear he was washed overboard by the waves! Is he on the ship? Is he all right? Has something befallen him? Father, Father!" she cried hysterically.

"Hortensia, Hortensia? My daughter!" came the pained voice of her distraught father some distance away.

"I am over here, Father!" They ran towards each other and embraced joyously, both happy just to be alive after this ordeal at sea.

Another Spanish lady was beside herself with hunger and exposure. She raised her slender-fingered hand to her left breast and fainted into the arms of the interpreter. The doctor came to her aid immediately.

"Quickly! Get some more wet cloths from Mr. Teely so we can cool her fevered brow to bring down her fever," said Loyster to a passing sailor.

The lady's forehead was covered in beaded sweat. Her cheeks were taking on a deep pink, almost red, appearance.

"She has fainted from heat, exhaustion and exposure to the elements," said the doctor, with a look of concern. "Take her into the shade! Apply cool cloths and sheets over her body. She needs attention and shade. And be quick about it!"

"Aye, aye, sir, right away!" Mr. Hilbert, another crewman, replied obediently. The heavy-set, hirsute gunner, presently acting as nurse to the Spanish patient, carefully lifted the lady into his arms and deposited her onto a makeshift mattress on the aft deck. He scurried back as fast as he was able to the surgeon's quarters for white sheets to help cool off the patient.

Other unconscious and hitherto forgotten passengers had begun to regain consciousness and were now moaning in discomfort.

I learned all this news, both about the ostrich and about the Spanish lady, the other passengers and the apothecary, much later. In the meantime, I had been lost during and after the ostrich incident. I had inadvertently been locked into one of the officers' cabins after having been sent to restock some supplies of dried fruit and port wine for the captain's quarters, when the ostrich had begun charging about below decks. In order to keep the bird out of the captain's and officers' cabins, the first officer had locked up their quarters to prevent damage there. It would have created total havoc if the ship's charts had been torn up, ingested or befouled by this ungainly and unpredictable creature. I had pounded on the door to be let out, but evidently no one had heard me.

When all the noise and commotion had died down, I began with renewed vigour to hammer the inside of the cabin door with small yet determined fists, yelling at times at the top of my lungs, desperate to attract attention. As a last resort, I started kicking the door forcefully, alternating with each of my square-set, buckled shoes, to create as much noise as was humanly possible from one of such small physical stature.

After much pounding of fists and kicking of doors, my pleas were finally answered by the boatswain, Mr. Swanson, who had been sent by Doctor Loyster to seek out more medical supplies for the Spanish passengers. The boatswain approached the door. "Who's there?" he asked cautiously.

"It's me — Christopher!" I said, by now filled with fear and exasperation.

"Hold on, lad. I'll have you out o' 'ere in a minute," Swanson reassured me.

The sound of keys jangling in the lock was sweet music to my ears! The boatswain had opened the door immediately with a key suspended from a ring encircling his thick leather belt. Rescued at last, I fairly threw open the door and leapt into the arms of my rescuer, happy to have escaped from my confined quarters. I burst into tears of joy and laughed hysterically at the same time.

"There, there, lad. You'll be safe and sound now," said the boatswain, sympathetically and gently patting my back.

" 'ere's me neckerchief. Dry your eyes now."

"Thank you, sir," I blubbered, my eyes welling up with tears, this time out of gratitude. With a corner of the red cloth, I dabbed my red, swollen eyes, gently sobbing, still recovering from my traumatic experience. "That's the most frightened I've ever been in my life, sir. Thank you so much for rescuing me," I said most gratefully.

"I was so fearfully worried that I might never see my mother again!"

My heart ached at the thought of my mother not being there to comfort me, and I was overwhelmed with a consuming feeling of homesickness and abandonment after these long months at sea. I was brought out of my reverie of home and thoughts of England by the kind-hearted Mr. Swanson's voice.

"If ye're quite recovered now, lad, the captain wants yer on deck presently. He were askin' about ye a good hour ago. So be off with ye," he said, gently but firmly. I felt suddenly foolish, knowing that other seafarers no doubt felt the same sorts of homesickness and longing as I did. I learned later that he had a son about the same age as I at his gabled house in St. Ives in Cornwall, awaiting his homecoming. The boatswain had three other grown sons and a daughter as well. This would be his last voyage; he was nearing four score years. This was old in terms of anyone in these times and even older for an old salt at sea.

Having sprinted out of the hold as fast as possible after my forced confinement, I soon forgot my own troubles. I was swept up in the pandemonium on deck, observing Doctor Loyster, who now proceeded to examine each of the strangely dressed people lying on the deck.

A few crew members from the *Vigour* appeared to be standing guard over and or attending to the needs of the more injured strangers. Wrapped in moistened bandages, they seemed a little like mummies from Egypt, images of which I had once seen at the White Horse Inn as woodcuts in a travelling bookseller's volume.

At first, I was utterly bewildered by all the comings and goings-on, what with all the frantic activity of the crew tending to the many stricken people who were scattered about the deck. They had been shuffled into every shaded spot. Who were all these strange people? What were they doing here? Where was the captain? Why were they wearing all these strange-looking garments, the like of which I had never seen before in my village or my limited travels in England?

I was roused from my thoughts by Doctor Loyster's voice. "You, there, cabin boy, find my assistant Mr. Teely. Tell him he must go to the stores room and the infirmary on the *Vigour* and bring enough sheets and water for all the people on deck, as they must be seen to immediately. You, in turn, will then assist Mr. Teely in carrying out his duties minding my patients."

In my semi-dazed state, I instantly forgot about reporting to the captain. "And be quick about it, lad," was the surgeon's last instruction before I disappeared below deck to find Dr. Loyster's assistant.

Below deck, I heard Mr. Teely talking to the ship's artist about our ship's doctor having become an expert on tropical diseases after his voyages had taken him to the South Pacific, Central America and other southern climes. Dr. Loyster was an invaluable member of our expedition.

I hastily greeted Teely and informed him of the physician's orders. We soon reappeared on deck, now laden with so many folded sheets that I could scarcely see over top of the stack I was burdened with. The doctor's assistant was visibly straining under the weight of two extremely large wooden buckets of water, which sloshed and spilt with every measured step. The veins and muscles in his arms and neck bulged out under the strain.

We soaked the sheets in clear water from one of the barrels used by the cook for collecting rainwater for washing and meal preparation. Teely also returned quickly with Loyster's black leather doctor's bag and instrument case.

The unconscious passengers' sunburned skin was covered with these wet, soothing sheets, and the good doctor applied salves from his medical bag. The patients, now beginning to rouse, were given fresh water to drink, with a sailor dispensing the life-giving liquid from a black iron ladle. They had become quite dehydrated after lying on the deck in the hot sun. The plan was now for the Spaniards to be taken to the closest port for provisions and water to restock their own ship so they might continue their journey to Spain.

Ten Spanish invalids remained unconscious lying on the deck, still oblivious to the world. They had been found at the entrance to the lower deck, where they must have been exposed to the worst of the fumes.

The two ships remained broadside to each other, linked by grappling hooks and ropes, just as when the *Santa Teresita* was first boarded. Both vessels were at anchor to stop them from drifting to and fro. Supplies could be transferred from one ship to the other with great ease. Fortunately, the gods had been smiling on the Spaniards this day, since they had been rescued from being adrift in unfamiliar and uncharted waters. The doctor found that the majority of passengers who had inhaled the fumes were in no medical danger.

"Beyond a doubt, the most afflicted patients shall be fully recovered in about two days," the doctor informed the Captain.

"Thank you, Doctor. As usual, you have done an exemplary job in treating your patients," replied Captain Salisbury.

"My only worry is there will be a shortage of food with these extra mouths to feed. We will have to put into port as soon as possible to restock our own stores with water, dried meat, fresh fruit and vegetables, as we are running out."

A few seamen were spared from the *Vigour* to help with sailing the Spanish ship, whose crew was short by three men until all had recovered from their misadventure. When the ships raised anchor and again put out to sea, the two ships stayed within view of each other to avoid any further problems that might complicate their voyage. Captains Salisbury and Alvarez agreed that they would sail together. This was a distinct case of there being strength in numbers. They could protect each other in case of attack by pirates or privateers or whatever man-made or natural disaster presented itself. They would part company when the patients were completely recovered and the *Santa Teresita* no longer required the services of the *Vigour* and her officers and crew.

After we had finished our errands and tasks for the day, there was a time when the young baker Simon Crudgely and I would spend an hour or so on the aft deck in conversation, regaling each other with stories of our separate adventures. Though about six years separated us and though we had greatly differing physical appearances, we found that we shared a similar outlook on the world.

The young lad had a comical bent, which sometimes manifested at inopportune times, as when he felt vexed by the actions of his superiors in the course of his daily work and ship's routine. On many occasions we'd meet, after what seemed to be an endless day of chores and errands, to exchange observations of our new life at sea and how our masters were treating us. We would discuss going home to England, since we had lived only a few miles from each other. We would burst out laughing in the dark on the mid-deck, and would have to quickly stifle it to avoid detection by the sailor posted for night watch duty.

5. A disloyal sailor plots mischief

FOR EIGHT DAYS we were becalmed at sea without wind in the sails, and the weather had warmed considerably. The men soon became listless, tired from the oppressive, sweltering heat. They cooled off during the day by jumping into the ocean every few hours, as only in this way did the heat become somewhat bearable.

It happened one evening when I had been tossing and turning in bed that I awoke fitfully from a rather silly dream of my mother's cat, Toffee, knocking back a pint at the White Horse Inn. I was worried and homesick, and being a dutiful son, I felt responsible for somehow helping mother to relieve her financial woes. Again and again I wracked my brain thinking of how I might help her upon my return home. I was determined to offer her my meagre wages, as I felt it was the least I could do to help her in her time of need.

My mother was the kindest and gentlest person I had ever known in my short life in this world. I wished that Captain Salisbury would find Blackbeard's legendary treasure, rumoured to have been buried on Blackbeard's Island. Under the terms of our employment, everyone was to benefit from the booty if any part of this fabled vast treasure was found. This would help my mother's financial situation to no end.

Blackbeard had supposedly buried his enormous treasure troves on several small islands, to avoid putting all his eggs in one basket, so to speak. That way, if some of his treasure were to be discovered by other pirates or privateers, he might still have more hidden elsewhere.

As I lay restlessly in my bunk, I often heard the bells rung in the dark for the change of watch. The beds were so small that most of the men could only sleep in them sitting up or with knees bent. Being of rather smallish stature, I did not find the beds uncomfortable. Many of the men, however, preferred stretching out whilst sleeping in hammocks slung from the ships' timbers.

Habitually, when I could not sleep, I would take the night air on the foredeck. This would calm my mind, and the evening constitutional would ease my fitful sleeps and troubled mind. To ease this restlessness, I decided to walk on deck again tonight.

Careful not to wake sleepers, I gently opened the door of my cramped little cabin and closed it quietly behind me so as not to wake the two sleeping sailors in their hammocks suspended from the ceiling. I quietly and carefully picked my way up the ship's ladder to the upper deck, again trying to avoid waking other crew members, many of whom had only been able to catch a precious few hours of sleep, what with the oppressive heat as we awaited blessed relief with any wind. The constant sun beating down on their heads created a bit of a daytime torpor, which was not conducive to a good night's rest or to working on deck.

Being from the British Isles for the most part, our shipmates had seldom experienced such heat, which rendered some of them virtually useless for many of their varied duties. I had suggested sailing at night while the air was cooler, but the Captain, with his years of experience, thought this to be a dangerous practice for ships and men alike, and thoroughly disagreed.

Stepping on deck one evening, I noticed a lantern swinging on the aft deck from the port side of the ship. It seemed as if it was suspended in midair, floating in the darkness. I looked closer to see if my eyes were playing tricks on me.

Instead, I saw a distorted visage of a sailor in the sickly, pale light of the lantern. I had never seen anything of this nature since the voyage began.

What was that on the horizon this time of the morning? Was it possible? I rubbed my eyes with disbelief. I saw a second light far in the distance on the horizon. Could it be? Another ship so close at hand, but sailing undetected by us? It sent a shiver down my spine. Perhaps it was a pirate ship fast approaching us in the night, or a merchant transporting slaves to the New World, bent upon capturing another prize to accompany their ill-gotten goods.

My suspicions were further heightened when I saw what appeared to be the same floating lantern wending its way along the deck approaching the ship's wheel. In the glint of the faint light from the lantern, I saw, dressed in nearly invisible black clothing, the dark, evil-looking face of Ishmael Kratz, contorted with malice.

Kratz must have been signalling the other ship at that moment. He extinguished the lantern quickly as I watched him in the darkness. Kratz had quite regularly taken the night watch, so I surmised that he might even have been doing this sort of signalling before, as part of his nightly routine.

I remained with my eyes transfixed, watching him, undetected. After a minute or two, I quietly slipped down the steps towards my cabin.

I knew I must warn the captain and my other shipmates immediately of this potential foul treachery brewing aboard the *Vigour*. Kratz must have been intimately acquainted with the crew members of the other ship in order to send messages by lantern to them. What was he telling them? How long had this treachery transpired without anyone's knowledge?

My mind flew hither and thither, in a thousand directions. I imagined the *Vigour* being boarded and overcome by bloodthirsty, cutthroat pirates swinging from the mainsails clenching knives between gaping teeth, putting everyone in sight to the sword. I was paralysed with fear as the urgency of the situation overtook me, but I had to remain rational and logical.

How many of the crew were part of this treachery, I wondered. Who could be trusted? I knew that Captain Salisbury was beyond reproach and that I could put my faith in him implicitly; indeed, I now remembered, as the lengthy discussions between my mother and him had revealed, that we were in fact distant relatives.

My feet barely touched the stairs, and my hand quickly glided along the handrail as I ran below deck to warn the captain of the imminent danger facing us all. I fairly flew to Captain Salisbury's great cabin and pounded furiously on his door.

"Captain, Captain, open the door, please! We are in great

danger!" I whispered hoarsely. My distress was great; I was gasping for air, being filled with anxiety at the prospect of being attacked by ruthless, bloodthirsty pirates at any moment.

The captain flung open the cabin door to face me in my state of obvious agitation. Salisbury was noticeably surprised at seeing me in the wee hours of the morning.

"I thought you might have been Mr. McCaury or Mr. Kratz. They're on watch duty till the morning. What are you doing up at this hour of the night? Shouldn't you be in bed? Are you ill? What seems to be the matter?"

"I'm not sick, sir. I'm afraid there is trouble on deck, sir."

"What is it, Christopher?" asked the captain, his teeth clenched tightly, answering tersely though visibly tired, wishing to be freed from this situation as soon as possible so he could resume sleeping the sleep of the just.

"Captain, we're being followed by a pirate ship! I saw their lantern light on deck in the distance, from the aft deck!" I blurted out, my face drawn and pale, whilst talking what must have appeared to be gibberish, all bursting out as fast as was humanly possible.

"What the devil are you talking about?" Salisbury asked, with total incomprehension. I think he had misgivings as to the state of my mind at this time. "Explain yourself, young man, at once."

"I was walking on deck when I saw Kratz signalling another ship with his lantern," I said matter-of-factly.

"What? What other ship? You know we're far from shore, in the middle of the Atlantic, Christopher!" the captain said, incredulous at this revelation.

"We've seen no ships for days! Where is the so-called other ship?" the captain growled in a tone uncustomary for him, growing more impatient and angry by the second. "If you're spinning me some sort of yarn, you'll be dealt with most severely, young man."

"Are you ill or delirious? Do you have fever?" he continued in rapid succession, shaking his head slightly back and forth, his eyes widening in disbelief and the furrows in his forehead becoming more pronounced than ever. "What evidence do you have of this, to make such accusations?" asked Salisbury, his eyebrows arched, gazing straight into my eyes.

Salisbury was concerned that I had succumbed to the effects of the tropical sun or some rare tropical disease. He was on the verge of awakening Doctor Loyster when I blurted out with almost uncontrollable emotion: "Come with me, captain! I'll show you! I don't have any time to explain!" At the very least, I suppose, Salisbury thought it was best to humour me in the escalating situation.

The captain reluctantly threw on a wine-red velvet robe over his beige nightshirt and followed me to the upper deck. As we stealthily approached the top step of the stairs, we saw Kratz, caught in the act, still signalling with his lantern. It sent a shudder down our spines. The captain looked at me in disbelief and with a deep sense of personal betrayal as another lantern on the horizon responded to the signal.

"You're absolutely right," he admitted. "I'd not have believed it, had I not seen it with my own eyes," the ship's master continued, as quietly as was possible under the circumstances. "We must go below deck before we're discovered, or we'll be undone," he whispered, almost below his breath. We then disappeared into the hold and returned as quickly as was possible to Captain Salisbury's cabin, which still had a taper burning on his charts table to light our way about the room.

"Sir, why are they following us?" I inquired, in guileless innocence. "We don't have any treasure to speak of, at least not yet."

"You tell me, lad, and we'll both know, Christopher!" he answered tersely, totally puzzled by this most recent turn of events. "What could possibly be afoot? What is Kratz up to?" the captain mused to himself, though audibly. Then, still *sotto voce:* "How could we have been so foolish as not to have noticed this before?"

"Maybe Kratz and the other ship's crew members are keeping informed of our whereabouts so as they can follow us, undetected, at a distance," I offered excitedly, though with fear and trepidation, my mind racing at my realization. "That way, when we find the treasure, they will attack us, and steal it from under our very noses after they've done away with us."

"That sounds about right, Christopher. You have the instincts, and insights, of a seasoned sailor," the captain said, promptly agreeing with my suggestion.

What were we to do? These people, whoever they were, were following us day and night. They were obviously up to no good.

"We'll have to defend ourselves at all costs. It is fortunate that we came across the *Santa Teresita*. We will join forces with the Spaniards, or at least the healthy ones, and face the villains together. It seems that an ill wind has blown this ship our way. It also appears as if someone else must have known of our plan to search for buried treasure on Blackbeard's Island, Christopher. These types of intrigues sometimes take on lives of their own. It only takes one loose and flapping tongue. Kratz must have found out about our plans in London."

All of a sudden, Salisbury came to the realization that the mysterious person he had seen galloping into the moonlight at the White Horse Inn when we had first become acquainted must have been no other than Ishmael Kratz! "How could I have been so stupid? I knew that I had seen his face somewhere before, but I just couldn't place it. We must act immediately," said the captain, with renewed concern in his voice.

For the time being, Captain Salisbury was at a loss for words. It was as if we were both transfixed with fear, unable to move, as the traitor continued with his rounds on deck, unaware that we had witnessed his heinous deed. "Come to think of it," the captain whispered almost disbelievingly under his breath. "I did catch him in my cabin on the day of our departure!"

"He was in my cabin without permission when we were docked in London," continued the Captain, "and when I asked him what he was doing here, Kratz told me he had seen a rat entering my quarters through an open window. How was I to know he was plotting against us?" Outside, I heard the shuffling of Kratz's feet as he approached the Captain's cabin, no doubt hiding in the shadows but straining to hear our conversation through the door, deaf as he was in his left ear since having been a gunner manning the cannons in a sea battle.

"I guess the only rat was Mr. Kratz," I suggested quietly. Salisbury ignored my remark.

"Yes, it all makes perfect sense now," he continued. "I was wondering why our owner's sailing orders seemed to have been tampered with. They looked rumpled, and the seal had been broken before we raised anchor in London. I had dismissed this thought, since I do have a ship to run here. Yes, yes! It all makes sense now! We don't have a moment to lose! We must move quickly and decisively to quell this planned mutiny if we are to save our lives. We must devise a divide-and-conquer plan," the Captain concluded abruptly.

Kratz eventually appeared before us, dishevelled as usual, though with a touch more malice than before, or so I fancied, in his eyes. The sailor pretended that one of the lines had snapped off and that he had observantly noted this. Though Captain Salisbury thought this explanation unlikely, especially in the dead of night, he played along with the charade and told the traitor to secure the line as well as he could tonight and that the morning watch would make proper repairs in the daytime.

Noting Kratz's easy ability to carry off a barefaced lie, I recalled his earlier efforts to incite fear among the men with his false stories of Captain Salisbury's supposed plan to abandon some of them on Blackbeard's Island after we had recovered any treasure that might be found there.

I now believe he had deviously fabricated these lies because he had wanted to foment some sort of mutiny before our sturdy and well-provisioned vessel reached Blackbeard's Island. His plan must have been that when they met up with Old Blacktooth, his partner-in-crime from previous pirate expeditions, they would have the physical labour necessary to claim the island's vast treasures themselves.

When Kratz returned to his post, Salisbury instructed me to summon immediately a short list of men in whom he knew he could repose the utmost confidence, quietly awakening each trusted individual in turn so as not to arouse any suspicions among the others, as the loyalties of some of the others might be subject to question. First I was to send two men onto the deck to watch Kratz and report any further actions on his part, so that he could not take us by surprise before we were ready to confront him.

When we were finally assembled in Salisbury's quarters, the Captain informed us all of the imminent danger we faced. To a man they were all stunned and shocked to learn of their dangerous new predicament. The captain addressed his loyal crew and instructed them quietly so that Kratz and any fellow conspirators would not and could not overhear us. Who knew if any pirates from the other ship had already boarded our ship on a previous night and were even now lying in wait to ambush the loyal crew? It was only a matter of time before we would meet them face to face, with the help, of course, of the traitorous Kratz.

"The quartermaster will issue firearms to each of you: two muskets, ball and powder to make ready in case we will have to discharge them this evening. Now make haste to the stores deck. Then quietly return to your hammocks, without raising the alarm, and conceal your weapons on your person!" said the captain in a low voice. After the worried men left to quietly collect their arms, Salisbury addressed me as I stood next to the chart table, trying to determine our direction of travel.

"Christopher, you can stay here with me for the time being,

as I require your help. Also I will lock you in my cabin for your own safety if fighting erupts, since you've never been involved in anything as dangerous as a mutiny or fight at sea."

Salisbury continued to explain his plan of action. "I will go on deck, under the pretext of taking the night air from not being able to sleep. I will be vigilant and observe if this other ship is still following us. We will not attempt to overpower him, since the other ship may detect trouble if it does not receive any signals that their crew may be expecting. They may even attempt to overtake and board us sooner than they had planned." The thought of this filled me with dread.

"We can't risk a full-scale confrontation, since we don't know the size of the force arrayed against us, nor do we have enough men for defence. We must remain undetected until the matter can be resolved in our favour — of course, with as little blood spilled as possible. Be vigilant," the Captain concluded, with an understandably worried tone in his voice. Salisbury spoke to me as he might address his own son. He felt he could confide in me as a youth of ready wit who, he said, possessed "intelligence and understanding" beyond my short life.

"I will, Captain Salisbury," I replied. "You can count on my loyalty always, sir. I am ever at your beck and call."

Slipping back to my cabin on the port side of the ship, I lay restlessly in my bunk, anticipating being called away at any moment. I reflected on the day's intrigue and tried to prepare myself for whatever lay ahead.

The captain in his cabin loaded his own pistol with ball and powder, intending to ready himself for any unwanted encounter with Ishmael Kratz or with the mysterious ship shadowing us.

6. Fire!

TWO DAYS LATER, both Salisbury and Alvarez had been carefully scanning the horizon for some time in the direction of our wake, when they finally spotted the ship to which Kratz had been signalling. The shadowing ship's captain had perhaps sailed closer to us than previously, in order to be in position to receive another night-time signal from the treacherous Kratz. Through his telescope Salisbury peered at the bow, trying to make out the ship's name, but the captain couldn't read it at the great distance that still separated the ships.

Then the Spanish captain asked to take a look through the telescope. Excitedly, he said: "I know that ship! I recognize the way they have rigged the sails. She is the *Contessa*. They tried once, on a previous voyage, to attack my ship, but we repulsed them with our cannons. They were unable to board us but were able to escape us before we could sink her. They are terrible pirates, and we must try to avoid them."

Knowing the identity of our pursuers crystallized our good captain's determination. Having finally decided to confront Kratz,

Salisbury awoke me that night and quietly crept on deck, hiding in the shadows to closely observe his behaviour a little longer. I had been watching as well, remaining by the forecastle whilst shadowing the captain. I did not want to be separated from my benefactor and protector for any length of time, more especially as he was facing immediate peril with Kratz. I remained hidden to avoid being detected and to stay out of harm's way; I was also in a position to come to the aid of the captain, if need be, with a truncheon. A lad of my small proportions was, of course, going to be of only limited use in rescuing anyone.

Salisbury again saw Kratz traitorously signalling the other ship following them. The other ship responded immediately with more flashes of light from its lantern.

Ishmael Kratz must have passed on to the captain and sailors aboard the *Contessa,* the ship that had been following us at a distance, the details of our sailing coordinates and plans by means of signalling with a lantern from the deck of the *Vigour* during his night watch. This way he maintained close contact with his confederates, while they remained undetected. Kratz would steal into the captain's quarters to find out the ship's course and location for the upcoming two days. Every night at the change of the night watch, Kratz would pass this information on to them by signalling from the quarterdeck. That way the ship could secretly shadow the *Vigour* and the *Santa Teresita* at a great distance, knowing our whereabouts yet still hidden by the black skies and water. On moonlit and starry nights, the vessel would remain out of sight, then catch us up near enough to receive Kratz's signal.

"Stop, you fiend! Traitor! Blaggard!" hissed the captain as

he leapt out of the shadows and tried to wrench the lantern from his traitorous hand.

Kratz drew back his lantern hand defiantly. "You won't take me alive, you fool! You won't send me mates off course, you won't, not for the life of me!" he vowed, swearing an oath at the captain, his contorted, corrupt, distorted face bathed in the sickly greenish rays of the lantern light.

Salisbury lunged to grasp the blabbering fiend's lantern, inadvertently knocking the lantern out of his hand. It landed on the deck, breaking the glass cover into a hundred pieces, spilling a small amount of oil from the reservoir onto the deck. Almost immediately, from where the oil from the lantern had spilled out, fire started to spread across the tarred deck. Both men continued their heated fisticuffs until the captain landed a deciding blow to the chin of the traitor, knocking him temporarily senseless to the deck. Kratz lay sprawled on the wooden plank, oblivious to the world and the effects of his incendiary deeds.

Fire spread rapidly across the deck from where the lantern had landed. Captain Salisbury ran to warn his men, yelling "Fire!" at the top of his lungs. Many were still asleep in their hammocks. He ran to the hold and yelled again: "Fire, fire! All hands on deck!" The men had been sleeping fitfully on the mess deck, in the forecastle and below the gun deck in neat, tight rows, like bats in a cave. Rudely awakened, the sailors leapt from their hammocks and raced onto deck, leaving the hammocks swinging in differing directions as if a ghostly presence still inhabited them. To try to contain the fire, I soaked my coat in a rain barrel and dashed it repeatedly where I saw flames blazing; the men came to help, and did likewise.

Kratz must have regained his consciousness about then, because the next time I looked in his direction, he was no longer lying where Salisbury's blow had felled him. By now, however, everyone was occupied with fighting the fire, and we could spare no one to search for the treacherous Kratz. The Captain ordered the men to line up for a bucket brigade, so we could fight the fire in a more organized and effective fashion.

To try to extinguish the fire on the *Vigour,* Salisbury and I, whilst waiting for our fire-fighting crew to assemble, tipped over a huge rain barrel, which somewhat slowed the spread of the fire but did not succeed in putting it out. Most of the men had come up on deck in such a hurry that they'd had no time to put on shirts; others removed theirs to better tolerate the intense heat from the fire.

With beads of perspiration covering grimy faces and bodies, their faces red, sooty and sweaty and kerchiefs singed by the licking flames, the men formed a fire-line, lowering buckets into the sea, passing them up to the deck and handing them down the line to the fire. It was nearly extinguished after forty minutes of intense battling of the leaping flames, which had burnt partially through the lacquered mizzenmast and charred a large portion of the deck. Burnt and blackened planks, smoke still arising from them, hissed when the sea water was dashed upon them.

Kratz had slipped down to the crew's sleeping quarters, gathered his belongings and ransacked the captain's quarters till he found the map to Blackbeard's Island, which he hastily stuffed into a duffel bag. Kratz threw a sack of ill-gotten goods over his shoulder, nostrils flaring as he ran upstairs onto the deck of the ship. He would have seen the men still battling the fire, their faces exhausted in the flickering of the firelight. Instead of helping to fight the fire, though, he headed straight for a longboat, untied the ropes securing it and lowered it into the sea. He was not foiled in his escape efforts, since all the rest of us were fully occupied in dealing with fire flare-ups on the deck.

Kratz knew he must work quickly to avoid detection and capture. He quickly lowered the longboat, clambered down the rope into the boat and disappeared into the night. As far as any of us knew, we'd never see him again. Some suggested that Kratz had ended up in Davey Jones' locker, shot as an intruder as he tried to board his shadow ship in the dark of night; others said he was carried away by the spirits of the night and still sails the sea on a ghost ship, signalling with his lantern to a ship that never appears on the horizon. I did not take seriously any ghost stories that I had heard, and I thought that Kratz's fortune was pretty much in his own hands. Presumably, he had stocked his stolen boat with necessary supplies; despite his surliness, rumour-mongering and outright treasonable conduct, he was undoubtedly an accomplished sailor and had a fair chance to make good his escape.

Luckily, Kratz's theft of the map would not hinder us from reaching our destination. Before leaving London, our resourceful Captain Salisbury had carefully drawn up another copy of the map, which he had hidden in a desk compartment.

Meanwhile, the pirate ship had gained on us and was broadside to the *Vigour* within five minutes. One of the pirates, in tattered green clothing, was readying his grappling hook to board our ship.

Suddenly, the fire flared up again from a place I had

thought that it had been stamped out. Evidently, the fire had almost burned through the deck planks and now continued burning on the other side. Our situation would become quite dangerous if we could not bring the new flare-up under control. The weakened planks might collapse altogether, and the entire ship would soon be engulfed in flames. Fire was again licking up the mizzenmast when Salisbury, out of the corner of his eye, noticed the *Contessa* was now barely a few feet away. A pirate was glaring at him with a knife in his teeth, readying himself to board our disabled ship.

With complete presence of mind, I grabbed a piece of burning wood which had fallen close to my feet and threw it at the deck of the pirate ship, then quickly scooped up the remains of another oil lantern and threw it over for good measure, this time actually breaking open the remaining oil reservoir in the lamp's base and spilling the entire contents on the pirate ship. A fire on the deck of the rogue ship began to spread rapidly since there was much flammable material on deck, which appeared to be piles of old canvas, rags and such. These pirates were not the neatest of caretakers of their vessel.

"Push off, Mulligan, or we'll be burnt to a crisp by both these 'ere ships!" a pirate — who had only a single front tooth — screamed to his companion. Another dozen mangy-looking riff-raff appeared on deck to try to douse the fire, lowering leaky wooden buckets to fill them with sea water and quickly starting to quell their own blaze. We were free of the pirate threat, but not for long, I thought.

Captain Salisbury, in the meantime, still had to deal with a fire raging on his own ship. Daylight was approaching. The shades of night had passed. Not until sunrise was the fire totally extinguished. Dawn progressed from pitch-black starry skies to grey clouds to brilliant blue heavens. Tired and exhausted, many of them covered in black soot from head to toe from smoke and charred wood, the men stood before the captain. "Good work," he commended them all, with a sigh of relief.

He addressed the assembled crew. "You saved us from Davey Jones' locker, men. We'll have to put in to repair the ship's deck. There we can take on water and provisions; our stores are desperately low. There should be fresh fruit, as our supply of oranges has been depleted. We can't risk scurvy. It is critical that we locate a suitable place as soon as possible. Extra rations of rum will go to everyone for all your excellent work. This will slow our voyage to Blackbeard's Island, but that island is itself not far off. Better safe than sorry, as the common saying goes."

Part of the deck under the mizzenmast had burned away from the intensity of the fire, and burnt and blackened planks surrounded it. Other masts had been likewise charred with fire, with several of the all-important rigging lines burnt to a crisp. Small wisps of smoke still rose from the tarry, resinous deck, which had been tinder-dry in the absence of rain. Planks creaked under the broiling sun, and the fresh-water supply in the wooden barrels was nearly exhausted after our fire-fighting efforts.

The day following the blaze, the crew were instructed to swab the decks with sea water to remove loose soot and charred wood-debris from the deck as best they could, salvaging as much usable rigging, sails and wood as was possible, while the debris was thrown overboard into the briny waters. Captain Salisbury wanted the ship as functional as possible, even though they would have to limp into port under half sail, what with a mast having been severely damaged in the fire.

The first mate, Mr. Sullivan, took the ship's wheel during a seagoing service of thanksgiving. Captain Salisbury heartily complimented his men on their heroic and valiant efforts while he addressed his assembled crew. "A job well done, men," he said, his uniform and face covered in soot. "It is now Sunday morning. We will give prayers of thanks for our Queen, for our Government and for our families." Salisbury prayed for a safe voyage from this point on to Blackbeard's Island and for a safe return to England.

We were three days bearing on a course for Grand Canary Island when our prayers were answered. All the Spaniards had recovered, as Dr. Loyster had predicted, while sailors spared from duties aboard our ship were now manning the Spanish ship.

"Land ho to port!" came the excited announcement from the crow's nest.

Captain Salisbury placed his spyglass to his right eye to confirm the sighting. "Excellent, Mr. McTavish!" he replied with a burst of enthusiasm and energy which overtook him, reinvigorating and inspiring him anew with a sense of purpose and direction. The captain breathed an audible sigh of relief and announced, "We can now be no more than 30 nautical miles from the Canaries."

"I have not taken the noon sextant reading yet. How can you be sure of that?" asked the first mate.

"It is perfectly straightforward, Mr. Sullivan. Do you see the tops of the four main peaks of the mountain there?"

"Aye. That I do."

"From our chart we know that the centre peak is over 4,000 feet high, while our eye level is roughly five feet above the deck, which is itself 20 feet above the water level. We need only take the square root of our height above sea level and add it to the square root of the tallest mountain height, then multiply the sum by seven and divide by six."

Though Samuel Sullivan was an expert navigator, he'd not known this bit of navigational arcana. Still, he always appreciated mathematics, especially when it had such practical application. I did not pretend to understand the details, but I took note of our Captain's knowledge and the obvious respect his men held him in, and resolved to learn maths, trigonometry and celestial navigation whenever I might have the opportunity to do so.

Sailing to the north of Tenerife, the island with the highest of the four peaks, the captain could see the branches of the palm trees swaying in the breeze. Sailing closer, the white sandy beaches presented a strong contrast with the azure ocean. It was a beautiful paradise, which Salisbury had experienced on numerous occasions on past voyages in these waters just north of the Tropic of Cancer. A sheltered bay would serve as safe harbour to anchor the ship while we undertook the needed repairs.

Had he not been under such pressing circumstances and under normal conditions, he would have enjoyed the exotic scenery to its full extent and glory. This would have been the most perfect place in the world to live. All he and his men would have to do is to fish every day or so for sustenance and climb some trees to harvest coconuts for their milky liquid. Mother Nature would generously and kindly provide tropical fruits like papayas, mangoes, passion fruit and pineapples, which would be found in great abundance growing in the wild in the lush jungles. All their needs would be provided for with far more ease in comparison to their own cold, clammy British Isles. Except for the excessive heat of the midday sun, which might make the men wilt in their tracks, descended as they were from the Norsemen and Gauls of old, this was truly a paradise. As it was, this voyage had been fraught with danger and intrigue since its inception on the docks in Liverpool.

The *Vigour* would now be anchored for much-needed repairs and a refit. Physical examination revealed that the vessel had sustained much more structural damage to the gun-deck and bow than had been previously suspected. The ship's carpenter, William Bartlesby, and his apprentice would be kept busy for at least a week working 14 hours a day milling, steam-curving and planing lumber to replace the fire-damaged areas, and fires under the black metal tar pots would be kept boiling around the clock so that the thick liquid tar could be applied to seal all the cracks and gaps that had developed over time.

We had just completed the repairs and had begun taking on provisions and water for the short trip to Blackbeard's Island when a midshipman spotted a ship from the crow's nest. "Ship ahoy, Cap'n!" the lookout announced loudly but apprehensively. "There'd be a most curious looking ship starboard side flying the Jolly Roger — the likes of which I've never seen before, Sir," he announced, with obvious apprehension in his voice.

"What, not again! How is this possible?" the captain exclaimed, rolling his eyes in utter disbelief. I saw immediately that it was the same ship that had tried to attack us earlier when we had been battling the fire.

7.   Landfall on Blackbeard's Island

RESOLVING TO TRY TO AVOID another risky encounter with the pirate vessel, Captain Salisbury curtailed our reprovisioning before we had laid in all the water and food we would require, and we set sail anew for the other end of the island.

Captains Salisbury and Alvarez did an informal survey, peering through their spyglasses to detect events that might be transpiring ashore. Both captains had agreed that they would back each other's men up with the full force of their weaponry.

Suddenly, without warning, a black arrow adorned with feathers the colour of blood struck their ship, scarcely ten inches from the head of Captain Alvarez. He fell to the deck, shocked and temporarily disoriented, anticipating still more arrows.

"Everyone onto the deck!" Salisbury ordered frantically. "We are under attack. This poison arrow may belong to the dreaded Mati Mahi tribes, who are thought to be cannibals. We must sail from here immediately for the nearest safe haven."

Captain Salisbury promptly joined his counterpart on the deck. They lay on their bellies, dodging arrows flying past their heads. For a brief moment the air was filled with what seemed to be red-winged birds with long stick bodies. There was chaos on deck as everyone fled below deck to avoid the poison arrows. The ship was afire with the red feathers whistling like gusts of wind through the air around us.

Hundreds of the arrows stuck into every part of the deck and its walls, yet somehow struck no one. The captains decided that both ships would sail out of this port as soon as the tide rose sufficiently. It would be too dangerous for crewmen to row the ship out to sea since they would be faced with another likely onslaught of the "devil birds."

The crew shielded themselves in any armour they could find, trying to protect themselves from the attack of the hideous, venomous bird arrows. As the ships finally set sail from the unwelcoming port, the arrows lessened in numbers. The natives could still be seen on the shores shaking their long, deadly-looking silver-grey bows at them. Everyone breathed a collective sigh of relief as the fateful island disappeared from sight, and they thanked their stars that they had not become stew in the pots of their potential captors.

The crew and captain became desperate to find a more friendly and less inhabited island, teeming, they hoped, with game and fresh water, where the dangerously low provisions stores could be restocked and water could be taken on board.

The convoy sailed the entire day to avoid encountering the cannibals again. Surely, they thought, they deserved better than this.

After a day's sailing, another small island was spotted. Again the familiar "Land ho" was announced, to the relief of the thirsty, hungry passengers, crew and officers alike. Unfortunately, however, it was inhabited by some strange species of creature. They resembled dogs but were the size of Shetland ponies. Their unruly orange and heliotrope coats were frightful to behold. As the ship approached shore to find safe harbour, these beasts, numbering in the several dozens, lined the beach. They growled and snarled, displaying rows of huge, drooling, shark-like teeth. These unholy creatures had a wild look in their glazed eyes. Some of them leaped into the water, attempting to surround the ship, displaying their malevolently smiling jaws at the horrified onlookers. Fear and terror struck everyone to the depths of their souls. Were they going to be eaten alive in this hellish harbour? Aboard ship, everyone was tremulous. Captain Salisbury, fearing the worst, used semaphore flags to alert the *Santa Teresita* of the fate that awaited them on this monster-infested island. The other ship quickly altered course. The *Vigour* followed, everyone being greatly relieved at the decision not to drop anchor.

Children burst into tears as the adults tried, mostly without success, to calm their fears.

"What are these creatures? Have you seen the likes of these unholy, abominable creatures in your life?" said the shocked adults, both fascinated and repelled by the bizarreness of these unknown creatures.

Having sailed past five larger islands and a few smaller ones, several of them beautifully tempting to the men who were eager to once again spend time ashore, the Captain directed the

Vigour through a strait between two islands. Passing a collapsed volcano cone, where one side sloped precipitously into the sea, we tacked to port as we began circling the island. Three coffee-coloured barefoot mulatto men in dried-grass skirts appeared upon the beach at the ship's arrival off the island's turquoise waters, then disappeared behind the red-flowered hibiscus bushes around broad-trunked palm trees.

From the mid-ship deck Captain Salisbury observed green coconuts floating by port-side on the gently swelling waters amid the flotsam and jetsam, along with delicate white, pink and yellow plumeria flowers and a string of magenta-hued bougainvillea. Overhead flew a small flock of bright mauve, turquoise and blue parrots. Seagulls also squawked as if greeting them to their native island home.

"This bodes well, Mr. McTavish. Gulls so close to shore indicate abundant supplies of fish. We must make camp and cast our nets to catch fish for supper. Let's make haste so that the crew and passengers of both our ships are settled in for the night. We must rest when the opportunity arises."

The men broke into cheers. They had longed to plant their sea legs on land again, since it had been now nearly three months since they had first sailed from Liverpool, and their work on repairing and re-provisioning the ship had allowed them no relaxation. They were weary of the voyage and needed some well-deserved rest to recuperate from their strenuous, dangerous and constant seafaring duties.

Alas! This was not to come to pass. As the crew gathered on the port side of the ship, they saw the *Contessa* already moored on the northeast tip of the island. They were still further taken aback and disheartened to see that it was flying the pirate flag of the infamous Ann Bonny and Calico Jack.

The sailors looked at each other with shock and dismay in their weary eyes. Their happiness had been short-lived. Could this really be happening, after all they had been through together on this fateful voyage? Everyone was brought back to reality by the sound of musket fire and ungodly screaming originating from shore. They braced themselves for anything and everything untoward.

"Where is that shrieking coming from? I thought for sure we had evaded the pirates and that we'd be the only ones on this tiny Atlantic island," their leader said, disbelievingly shaking his head slightly from side to side. "All hands on deck!" ordered Captain Salisbury. "Issue a musket, gunpowder and ball for every able-bodied man and woman on the *Vigour* and the *Santa Teresita*. We must arm ourselves to the teeth. They may intend to trap us, Mr. Spikes."

"Yes, sir!" replied the quartermaster, anticipating that his services would be required momentarily. Captain Alvarez followed suit on his ship. The weapons and ammunition were issued and distributed in short order on both vessels. Together with Mr. Teely, I helped Mr. Spikes in issuing weaponry to our crew.

This *would* have to happen when we are in short supply of fresh water and provisions, Salisbury thought angrily. Aside from Lanzarote and the other islands they had already passed, the next closest land was the northwest coast of Africa. In the meantime, he knew he might be forced to engage unsavoury men, possibly pirates, in combat. Sometimes ignorance is bliss, even if it is for a short while. It allows the mind to regain its balance and strength with being lifted from harsh reality.

Crews and passengers alike breathed a sigh of relief when the ship finally anchored at a sheltered harbour on the leeward side of Blackbeard's Island. The longboats were carried on skids between the gangways, as was the normal routine, and lowered with ropes. Each of the longboats was armed with five able men who were excellent marksmen. I was brought on one of the boats to assist them and to serve as a messenger to keep the captain posted on his men's actions. They all carried muskets to defend themselves on the island in case of pirate attack. We knew not whether they might be sleeping on the deck of their anchored ship or lying in wait to attack us on this strange and little-known island.

A scream rent the air. The skies were darkening as grey storm clouds gathered quickly. Dusk was falling on the island. Though I gave no solid credence to the idea of ghosts, still I could almost feel the ghostly spirits of former pirates and buccaneers descending upon the island. It sent a chill up my back, and the hairs on my neck stood on end as we picked our way along the rocky beach. We half expected a revived Blackbeard or Henry Morgan to come leaping out at us dressed in rags and haunting the very spot where we stood. Some of the men were tense in the anticipation of conflict or unnerved by their active imaginations, since the very name or thought of the recently decapitated Blackbeard was enough to make the most seasoned sea dog tremble.

Our fine captain tried to reassure the men, but the men's agitation only increased when they came upon a skeleton planted in the sand with its arm pointing to the western part of the island, as if warning us of what dangers lay ahead. The clothing on the skeleton was tattered, with the remainders of a felt hat stuck in an eye socket. A rusted dagger protruded from the skeleton's ribs. The sight of it struck terror into several crew members, and Jonathan Mollet gave voice to their fears.

"Captain, Captain! I beg of you, go back before it's too late!" he ranted, cringing at the sight of the skeleton and gnashing his teeth. The crew felt that the skeleton was an evil omen, and many wanted to turn back without any further delay.

"Pull yourselves together, men! Fear the living, not the dead. You're in better stead than he be!" admonished the Captain. "We must find fresh water before sunset, or we'll be completely out. The barrels are almost dry. The first man that finds fresh water will receive double rations of rum. Now get on with it before I have to take the "cat-o'-nine-tails" to you."

Normally Captain Salisbury was of a kindly nature and disposition, but he would occasionally talk roughly to bolster the crew's courage, since they were for the most part an unlearned and superstitious lot. The heat and the never-ending series of exhausting adventures were finally taking their toll both mentally and physically. He valued his men greatly, since the whole success of the voyage was literally in their hands. He lived or perished according to their great skills as seamen, and his words seemed to calm even the timorous Mollet.

"Captain, beggin' your pardon, sir," interrupted Marvell Dickins, a regular seaman. "Where should we be lookin' for water?"

"Make for the areas of the highest elevation, where you may more easily spot a stream. From a high point we can also survey the island to determine the exact location of the pirates. I do not wish to confront them unless it is absolutely necessary, and I want you to fire only if we are fired upon. Hopefully their suspicions have not yet been aroused." The Captain's concern for his men's welfare was once again obvious. "You have strict orders to stay together at all times. There's strength in numbers, men. We must not become separated, or this will undermine the safety of our voyage," he said, firmly and resolutely.

8. Monkeys, baboons and little green people

A FTER MOLLET HAD CALMED DOWN from the quite frightening sight of the ghoulish skeleton, we climbed to higher ground on Blackbeard's Island and finally came upon a waterfall. Here was surely enough water thundering down from the mountains to satisfy the needs of the *Vigour*, the *Santa Teresita* and all their crews. We filled four casks and manoeuvred a cart with the water supply down to the beach. How we wished we had some oxen with us to help out, or even a few of the goats from our ship, but our able-bodied seamen surely proved their mettle that day.

Back on the beach, we came upon a startling sight. About one hundred monkeys and baboons of every exotic colour — ranging from milky tangerine, magenta, mauve, lime and every combination and description — spontaneously appeared, pouring out of the jungle underbrush.

To our great surprise, the rainbow-coloured baboons and monkeys soon delivered a large quantity of tropical fruit. The abundant fruit included mangoes four times their normal size, starfruit, papayas, pineapples, dragon fruit and many multi-coloured coconuts; the whole had been placed in a mound on a blanket which had been left carelessly on the beach under a palm tree. Breadfruit trees were common and in plentiful supply on the island. There were also some exotic fruits that they had never seen before, in many odd colours and shapes, some like daisy flowers as big as a man's hand. Other fruits had normal shape but were of an odd pastel colour and varying shades of yellow, pink and emerald-green, perhaps owing to the equally odd-coloured soil and rocks on the island, which were darker hues of their tropical fruit counterparts. There was enough to feed an army if need be — crew members and passengers alike. These were exotic fruits that the captains, crews and passengers had never seen before in their lives and which they viewed with initial suspicion and concern, some beset with dark worries of illness and of food poisoning from its consumption.

The monkeys and baboons carried huge coconuts filled with sweet milk to quench the thirst of the sailors, along with papayas, starfruits, pineapples twice their normal size and other exotic fruits hitherto undiscovered by the Europeans. Besides the adults carrying fruit in their large multicoloured hands or balancing them on their well-formed heads, infants of varying sizes also carried similar, smaller fruits more fitting to their size and strength. They were helping their parents and other family members in this laudable effort to feed the tired, thirsty and hungry humans.

All the stranded people on the beach were dumbfounded and transfixed by the sight. Their jaws dropped, and children stopped in their tracks, frozen in a combination of fear, awe and disbelief. A mauve and light-pink baboon, who appeared to be the leader of the troop, approached one of the "ladies of quality," whose mouth appeared to be frozen open in shock. The baboon carefully slipped off the woman's wide lavender silk shawl, perhaps having been drawn by its similarity to the monkey's own colouration, and then proceeded to spread out the shawl on the sand in front of the petrified woman. The apes, along with their equally colourful children, then took the fruit they had brought and spread it out on the "picnic blanket" in neatly organized piles sorted according to the type of fruit they had picked and offered the fruits to their human guests. Another turquoise ape demonstrated how to strip away the husks and open the coconut at its soft spot with a sharp pointed stone. By holding up the face of her little ape baby and pouring milk from the broken coconut into its mouth, the mother ape showed the people how they could relieve their thirst with the precious, life-giving liquid.

Amidst all these goings-on, the people remained stunned, almost a captive audience, as it were. It was, to them, an utterly incomprehensible and unbelievable occurrence. Having proved their kindness, generosity and compassion by stanching the sailors' and passengers' immediate hunger, the whole mob of primates promptly turned heel, in perfect unison, reminding the sailors of a disciplined army, and headed straight for the jungle from whence they had come.

The cooks, crew and the willing and helpful passengers soon offered to aid in the preparation of the copious quantity of fruit. The sheer abundance was astonishing. There was enough to feed the three hundred people for a good week. In a joint effort, the two ships' cooks and the volunteer food preparation crew concocted an exotic fruit salad, in an attempt to feed the hungry passengers and crew. The remaining fruit was stored in hammocks slung between two palms. Many other passengers and crew were taken aback by the appearance of the fruit salad and viewed their latest meal with a mixture of distinct awe, distrust and interest, since they had never seen any food like this before. As this was the only sustenance in their immediate vicinity, though, they would have to make the best of their immediate situation. Doctor Martinez, on the other hand, had seen such copious varieties of fruits before. When he boiled and cooled the fruit mixture, the stewed-fruit concoction took on a new appearance — purple with lime-green spots, and now a nourishing and tasty jam.

Two willing crewmen, hunger overtaking them, volunteered to try the mixture. When the remainder of the hungry people found that the two sailors had suffered no adverse effects, the remaining people began to sample this concoction, also without any observable negative reactions. Women and children were served first, and then the crew members were served last. They ate and drank the mixture out of their bowls.

"When's this ever going to end?" the red-headed cook. McCaffrey, moaned in his exhaustion, with sweat pouring off his brow in the midday sun as he ladled his new concoction into eagerly awaiting bowls. After everyone was fed, they set about dealing with the next task at hand, which was getting enough sleeping accommodations for the population, as the sun set on the beautiful golden, crimson and rose-coloured sky.

Later, when all the humans were resting after their repast, some on ship and some on shore, they were able to gather their collective thoughts to discuss the day's events. Some questioned their own degree of sanity. They felt as if their minds had been playing tricks on them, but their full bellies argued that they had been literally well served by the pastel baboons and monkeys. Who would believe this at home in the villages and cities in England? They would have thought they had all gone daft or something with the tropical heat.

"Fancy that!" "Did you see the likes of anything like that?" or "I couldn't believe my eyes!" echoed throughout the island and on the ships in the bay till the wee hours of the morning, when they had all drifted off to a well deserved sleep.

In the afternoon, Nixon, Spikes and I went out on a search party to try to locate a second, less remote supply of fresh water for all the new residents on the island.

Our provisions were being somewhat supplemented with birds shot by top marksmen from each crew, as the captains had formed hunting parties to help feed the passengers and crew. Due to the small size of the island, there were limited natural resources to draw upon. Breadfruit, discovered by an observant volunteer, was gathered by sailors and passengers deputed by the captains of their respective ships. We learned that breadfruit flour could be combined with wheat flour to make bread, and that the ripe breadfruits could be baked or roasted like potatoes.

The baboons and monkeys, we learned, had been able to provide us with so much fruit because the trees had yielded an especially large harvest this year, perhaps due to unusually heavy rainfall.

Captains Alvarez and Salisbury jointly instructed their men and passengers at the fruit feast spontaneously provided by our generous island hosts that under no circumstances was any harm to come to any of the apes or their infants, since these primates had been our benefactors in time of need. Indeed, we might well learn a lesson from this fine example of helpfulness, cooperation and willingness to share their abundance. We might even require the apes' help again on some other occasion, since we did not know what was in store for us on this little island.

In the evening we all supped again on fruit salad until we were fairly stuffed and satiated — all thanks to the kindness, consideration and great generosity of our monkey and baboon neighbours. Most of the women and children were rowed back to the *Santa Teresita* for the night. Dusk was falling rapidly, and a classic and beautiful pink-skied sunset welcomed them back to their ships.

Back on shore, similar sleeping arrangements were being made for the men. Just as Captain Salisbury was about to lay his head on his fluffed-up sea-grass pillow, the sound of wild war drums filled the air. Everyone woke up with a start in their makeshift beds.

"What now?" Salisbury wondered, his eyes rolling skywards. Just when he was starting to enjoy the evening calmness that descends over the night air when all are readying themselves for bed and the din of human activity is reduced, the drums began to get louder, as if the drummers were approaching their camp from about four hundred yards' distance. Salisbury and Alvarez bolted out of their makeshift beds.

"All men to arms!" they ordered their men.

"Issue every man a musket, ball and powder, immediately! What's keeping you, man?" Salisbury bellowed, striding quickly towards the quartermaster's munitions shed to make certain his orders were carried out swiftly and efficiently.

The captains and officers could not readily determine the direction of the beating drums. The sound seemed to surround them. I had been sleeping nearby in a small hammock slung between two stunted palm trees and was startled at the sound of the approaching drums. Eyes widening, I realized the gravity of the situation and wondered if we might be attacked at any moment.

"Captain, where are you?" I called, unsure of what to do.

"By the munitions shed, Christopher. Come here right now!" the English captain replied. I ran to him.

"Take cover in the shed. Don't come out until I give the order," Salisbury warned.

The drums were still approaching; they sounded as if they were coming from all sides and from the sky as well. All of a sudden, as quickly as they had begun, the drumbeats stopped.

In less than one minute, from luxuriant vines which grew all about us, hung perhaps two hundred greenish pygmies. With blood-red noses and bright yellow daisy-shaped hair piled high on their heads, they seemed to fill the heavens and the palm trees with their odd, flowerlike appearance. Each had a small gold drum attached by a strap to his shoulders, along with long, thin silver sticks which looked like they could double as short spears. Upon closer examination, orange circles around their eyes gave them a more fearsome appearance, as did their green and black, sharpened teeth. They resembled flying lizards. The pygmies slid down the vines at a breakneck speed into the midst of our group and started screaming and ranting at the top of their lungs at us — who were, from their viewpoint, unwelcome intruders.

By this time, everyone had been rudely awakened, even those sleeping on the ship, by their drums, odd appearance and antics. They swung their silver rods dangerously close to the heads of the people nearest them — in order to intimidate them, we thought. Their strange appearance and spectacular entrance caused widespread pandemonium. Everyone feared for his life and safety. The people on the beach ran in all directions trying to avoid the onslaught of the green invaders. From a safe distance, their antics might have proved entertaining and engaging, but in their midst, the passengers and crews alike were terrorized beyond belief. They were stunned and numbed with fear.

The frightful green creatures then proceeded to warble at the top of their lungs like large birds, while flapping their arms like the wings of oversized eagles or condors. Their behaviour became more and more bizarre, unpredictable and erratic, which seemed almost engineered to cause widespread panic and fear. Then, as suddenly as they had appeared on the scene, they all fainted, collapsing in a group swoon. They appeared as if they had gone unconscious with their eyes wide open.

The captains ordered their officers and men to bind and gag these unknown creatures with their arms behind their backs and to do so promptly, before they awoke from their trance. They would be less trouble thus pacified than ranting and raving. The pygmies were left where they had fallen on the sands, enclosed within a temporary wooden fence erected by the ships' carpenter and four apprentices.

Doctor Loyster, upon examination of these creatures' mouths, which were stained orange, determined that they were in an induced trance from consuming the leaves of the *coccadile* bush, which proved to be highly addictive and caused bizarre trance-like zombie behaviour. He also learned that the leaves the natives had consumed had been used in their ceremonies to induce a dream-like state in which these individuals could perform great feats of derring-do, with the superhuman strength and agility of ten men. They became almost invincible armies against their foes. When they finally awoke ten hours later, they were surprised and frightened to find themselves bound, gagged and confined to the beach.

In the morning we untied their bonds, and Loyster offered our prisoners some of the salad of fruit, since this would undoubtedly have formed a part of the pygmies' natural diet, They appeared as if they had lived on this island for some time and seemed to have an intimate knowledge of climbing trees.

The jungle people turned out to be ordinary human beings. Though small in stature, they had decorated themselves with colourful paint that glowed in the dark to frighten foes. For a time, the captives were subdued. Everyone, including the captains, officers and crew, breathed a collective sign of relief. All the women and children from both the *Santa Teresita* and the *Vigour* — with their servants, nannies and curious onlookers — approached the green pygmies. Their eyes widened as they saw who lay before them. These green persons were a source of great interest to the children, especially since they had never seen such people before. They bent over them to cautiously examine them with little, chubby fingers, curiously touching the natives' bright green-tinged skin when their nannies and mothers were not looking. Natural curiosity overcame them.

"Don't touch, Chesworth!" said a horrified nanny, suddenly appearing in her powder-blue afternoon dress. "You don't know where that little green man has been," she continued in a pronounced Yorkshire accent. "Flyin' around all those trees like regular monkeys. You don't want to catch anything, now," she continued. The green people, who had slept where they had collapsed, were stirring, groaning a bit, like drunken pirates after a carouse. All seemed to be feeling the ill effects of spirits drunk in quantity over a short space of time. The leaves they chewed may have been responsible for these unwanted side effects.

The captains, along with two senior officers, remained behind to discuss the fate of the gallivanting green people. They resolved that since they had not really harmed anyone, the pygmies posed little or no threat to the company, and the gates of the fence were opened to set them free.

Then the heavens opened up with a great deluge of summer rain, followed soon after by balls of lightning, which seemed to pursue them at every turn. They were too petrified to move, lest they fall victim to a ball of heaven-sent fire.

The lightning pursued them into the jungle, sending the passengers, crew, captains and their officers fleeing in search of safety. When the rain-drenched people reached the natural jungle canopy, one distraught lady's hair was still smoking from the effects of the ball of lightning. Her face was blackened on the forehead, cheekbones and her prominent nose, looking for all the world like a London chimney sweep. She was not only upset by this most unusual occurrence of nature's fury but was much affronted and offended by the laughing and tittering that met her when she finally reached her dry refuge. She looked comical because of her dishevelled appearance, since she had always tried to remain the epitome of style and fashion even at the most trying of times all through the voyage.

The lady was uninjured physically and did appear to be otherwise unscathed after her encounter. Her white dress now bore a wide black stripe down the middle of her torso and the back side of her garment now exposed her *derrière* — a rather drafty and indelicate situation which, since she was not greatly harmed, continued to occasion some amusement in the others.

"Maybe milady should stand under the leaky part here to extinguish that smoke in her hair," suggested her lady-in-waiting with a slightly amused smile.

"Also, ma'am, would you like my shawl to cover you?" her servant offered, casting her eyes discreetly in the direction of her mistress's *derrière* while trying to avert her eyes. The servant lady was trying to avoid as much social embarrassment for her mistress as was possible under the trying circumstances.

The torrential downpour threatened to uproot some large palm trees, which now lashed about violently in the wind. The unleashing of the watery torrents was even beginning to create dangerous flooding in the low-lying areas.

In the meantime, we observed the hundred or so colourful primates, thoroughly frightened by nature's fury, heading for the same protected area as the huddling humans now inhabited. The monkeys and baboons seemingly talked amongst themselves in their own language, gesturing all the while toward us with their long, orange, green and yellow hairy arms. We felt self-conscious at being eyed and discussed by the animated primates, who alternately showed their teeth and stuck out their tongues at us. It felt odd indeed to be outnumbered by monkeys and baboons. There appeared to be at least two or three hundred of them, of varying colours and sizes. They all seemed to live together mostly in harmony, with the occasional short-lived flare-up soon resolved with the loudest baboon winning the argument. We felt like aliens in a new and strange world.

The children, too, were both fascinated and taken aback by these unfamiliar goings-on. They had never experienced the likes of this before. The dripping-wet, multicoloured animals who had been their benefactors were hysterically screaming when they reached their intended refuge to find that their sanctuary was already occupied by the humans. The people froze in their tracks, no longer mindful of the animals' great generosity on the beach earlier.

They did want to avoid any confrontation with the beasts. The animals loomed very large, about seven feet high on average — some taller, others shorter, powerfully built and as wide as two men side by side.

Captains Alvarez and Salisbury had not had the time or presence of mind to arm anyone with muskets or guns before the downpour began. Hell hath no fury like a troop of wet baboons and monkeys running from lightning, as the terrified people were soon to learn firsthand. The enraged animals, acting out of irrational fear, began grabbing anything in close reach. They ripped small trees and shrubs from the ground and threw them at the humans, who by this time were also screaming in fear. The petrified men, women and children were pelted with coconuts, palm leaves, bark, branches, small rocks and even monkey feces, which flew by their faces and struck them.

"To the boats!" one of the clear-thinking crew members screamed in the thick of the mayhem, as the others, including Salisbury, Alvarez and their officers, were overwhelmed mentally and physically. The human constitution can only take so much distress and new stimulation before it shuts down altogether at the most inopportune of times. "Get out of 'ere now before they trample us!"

As the crewman started sprinting towards the beach, everyone — men, women, and children — followed suit, with the monkeys and baboons shaking clenched fists at them as they set off in hot pursuit.

Children screamed at the top of their lungs in terror at being pursued by the crazed primates. The older women and some elderly men followed suit, emitting most distressing sounds, since they were hardly able to keep up with the rest of the group. "Chesworth! Run, run, or they'll kill us!" said his wide-mouthed, hysterical nanny as she clutched the child's hand tightly, fearing a trampling by the stampeding adults.

The people reached the three longboats, which were lying in wait in the shallow water no more than three feet deep with their anchor ropes secured to huge rocks to stop them from floating away.

"Fifty people in each boat!" ordered Salisbury tersely. He had finally snapped out of his stricken state and had fully come to his senses. Once more he took charge of the situation: the evacuation of all passengers, officers and crew alike. The remaining children and their mothers were hoisted into the longboats first, and then the men clambered in. Finally, the last stragglers piled into their respective boats.

The sheer number of human beings entering the water had churned the ocean nearly white around the longboats. The monkeys and baboons were gaining on them and had made it to the water's edge, baring their teeth, drooling and screeching at the top of their lungs. They wished their human tormentors to disappear as soon as it was physically possible.

The men attempted to drive off their pursuers by swinging long oars at them as the enraged creatures attempted to board the vessels. The last crew members, who had been aiding the women and children, finally piled aboard and cut the ropes. The longboats were dangerously overloaded, since they were not meant to carry so many passengers at one time.

A lime-green and mauve-striped baboon had now almost reached one of the longboats and was attempting to sink it by rocking it up and down like a toy. It had almost succeeded; the boat was starting to take on water when the gunwale struck the baboon a glancing blow on its chin on the way up, thus knocking the animal out of the water and flinging it backwards into the waves. The baboon lay unconscious on its back floating in the water. Thankfully, it posed no further danger to the people in the longboats.

The crewmen started to row double-time, needing no encouragement or orders, as fast as their oars would carry them in the direction of their awaiting ships. Seated with their backs to the ships and facing the shore from which they had come, the oarsmen saw two other baboons come to the rescue of their unconscious mate, whom they quickly pulled to shore in a most compassionate fashion. The unconscious primate was then laid out prostrate on his back as others gathered around him touching him on the face gently and tenderly while shaking him lightly by the arms attempting to help him to regain consciousness.

At a safe distance from shore and out of reach of the incensed beasts, Salisbury repeated his order to continue rowing quick-style towards the ships. The people's eyes were riveted on the other baboons, some of whom were still charging into the water in hot pursuit even as the separating distance grew.

On shore, three hulking beasts rolled a long driftwood log into the water. Ten colourful beasts, all in shades of mauve, light pink and royal purple, then tried to jump onto the huge log, which promptly sank, as it had been extensively burrowed into by teredo worms. Our pursuers thrashed furiously in the water for a minute while trying to right themselves, but had trouble in synchronizing their efforts. They stood up again, only to have the log sink onto their ample toes. Some were now leaping around the water on one foot, screaming in pain and frustrated in their attempt at pursuit.

Meanwhile the overloaded longboats had little freeboard and nearly capsized on at least three occasions while returning to the ships. The monkeys and baboons on the sand continued their loud ranting and displays of anger, stamping their feet and jumping up and down haphazardly. The uproar continued until the three longboats had neared the ships.

Reaching our ships, the people boarded the vessels, which seemed to take an eternity, since the passengers took so long to clamber up the unsteady rope ladders, and some smaller children had to be lifted up in baskets at the ends of ropes. After this was accomplished, Captain Salisbury ordered the officers to call off each person's name to be certain everyone was accounted for. A similar roll call was also held on the *Santa Teresita*. That was the time they must have learned that I was missing.

Captain Salisbury quickly surveyed the longboats to look for me, but I had climbed a coconut palm for safety and was nowhere to be seen, and Salisbury scanned the shore of the island. Only then did he spot me at the tree-top near the shore; I was waving an arm frantically in his direction, knowing that any sound could jeopardize my existence if I inadvertently alerted the still enraged animals to my presence, who could and would in turn shimmy up the palm at a second's notice to attack me.

The captain breathed deeply as if bracing himself for the next turn of events. When was this going to stop, he worried. Salisbury did not alert the rest of the passengers immediately, but discussed it confidentially with his officers and men after all the people on board were settled for the night, to see what could be done to relieve my predicament. An attempted rescue could further endanger me by drawing the attention of the enraged baboons to my plight.

I, too, worried about if, and how, the captain and crew were going to rescue me. Perhaps they would plan my escape under the cover of darkness. I could only hope for the best as I watched the sun disappear on the horizon and as the silhouetted primates sauntered along the now moonlit beach. The moon was large and golden, like a harvest moon in Britain, adding beauty to the palm trees' gentle swaying in the evening breeze along the shore.

9. In a palm tree, I fear for my life

IN THE EARLY MORNING, after I had dozed off for what seemed only a few minutes, I awoke to find that my tree was now surrounded by large magenta and mauve jungle cats. They had certainly spotted me and were eyeing me menacingly, as I thought, for their luncheon or, possibly, their dinner. How could I escape from these dire straits, which seemed to thwart me at every turn?

At first I thought I was rescued from danger when a group of ten shouting natives, all painted in amazing lime-green metallic colours, appeared with spears and frightened off the cats. I soon realized, much to my chagrin, that I was in even more trouble than I had anticipated, as the men now gathered at the bottom of the tree, as if simply replacing the previous hungry jungle cats. I could not tell whether they had spotted me, but I could not help worrying that they might be cannibals. I certainly hoped not! Anyway, there wasn't much meat on my skinny arms and bony legs.

Meanwhile, in his ship's cabin on the *Vigour*, Salisbury was contemplating how he might rescue me. He was caught in a double bind. Should a party row back to shore expressly to rescue me, his virtually "marooned" cabin boy, thereby putting all his charges into potential danger? What was my good captain to do? Although I was hidden for the time being, out of view from the beady-eyed natives, I could not stay in the tree forever. The captain of the *Vigour* decided to err on the side of reason and the common good and was forced to leave me in my predicament until it might be possible to rescue me later. It was obviously a gut-wrenching decision, but he could not have made efforts to rescue me that night, since it could have jeopardized numerous persons on the ships in a possible armed confrontation.

Trapped in the palm tree, I sat crouched and shivering, hidden temporarily by the giant palm leaves. I fully imagined and expected the green people to discover me at any moment. I also revisited the prospect of being forced, kicking and screaming, into a cauldron of boiling water with subtropical vegetables and being stewed for dinner whilst the natives danced around, all brandishing their spears and licking their chops in anticipation of their next meal, namely me.

I had overheard stories from the old crew on the *Vigour*, who told of tales of cannibalism where native people found it an honour to partake of the flesh of people they held in high regard, since they believed that all the power, spirit and goodness of this individual would go into themselves and would become part of their being and soul afterwards.

I was relieved in my young mind, thinking these people would not hold me in high regard, since they didn't know me.

Though trying valiantly to dismiss these thoughts, I was still terrified beyond my wildest fears.

As a child trapped atop a palm tree far from the reach of my mother's love and protection, I felt frightened and alone. How would I make good my escape?

"Oh, no!" I exclaimed, as one of the natives started to shimmy up the tree with the sun glinting off his knife, held between pointed, sparkling-white teeth. Fearing an imminent attack, I nervously watched as I saw his huge, glaring eyes approaching me.

Spotting three large coconuts hanging within my reach, I proceeded to defend myself by pelting the native's head with them. The first one missed the mark, but the second one struck the jungle man squarely on the forehead, and he fell unconscious to the ground. The green man's head was partially buried in the sand where he landed. He squirmed and thrashed about until two other green men extracted him from the ground, to their evident relief. They all followed their eyes up the tree trunk to locate the source of their aggravation, with anger and revenge glittering in their eyes.

Had I not been in such fear for my life, this might have been a laughable situation. As it was, however, I remained frozen on the spot. All of a sudden, a spear sailed by my head, then another and another. I ducked to avoid them, bobbing my head from side to side. The shaft of the last spear thrown, however, finally delivered a glancing blow to my head, knocking me out of the tree. I fell like a rock, screaming all the way down, and was rendered unconscious when my head struck the trunk of the tree, before I landed, crumpled up in a heap, on the sand.

Finally stirring, I found myself surrounded by the jungle people, all seemingly aghast at what they had done. Thinking they had knocked some game animal out of the tree, they were most surprised that instead they had captured a young ruddy-cheeked English lad.

The green man who had knocked me out of the tree had run to the water's edge to fill a conch shell with salty water. He had returned and splashed my face with it, hoping to revive me. He bore an expression of care and concern, like a father for a son. Around him, inquisitive and wide-eyed natives peered at my face from close range, trying to determine the extent of my injuries. Although my temple throbbed where I had been struck, I had not sustained serious injuries — just a few scrapes on my knees from when I had landed in the hot sand.

A few of them, evidently not among the party of green men we had previously encountered, seemed to be determining which planet I had come from. Judging from their faces, it was evident they had never seen a white person before. They touched my arms and legs as if gently trying to rub off whatever pale powder or paint I might be covered with, while at the same time checking for obvious broken bones or serious scrapes. When they realized it was my natural colouration, they looked at each other furtively, surprised at this discovery. Their own wiry parrot-green, bright pink and canary-yellow hair, which stood about a foot off their heads and billowed softly in the gentle wind, made them resemble birds with gorgeous tropical plumage.

It was a great source of interest to myself, even in my dazed and weak state. I was still distracted by their handsome features, enhanced by their tropical colour schemes, which contrasted dramatically with their chocolate-coloured skin where it was not covered in lime-green paint. They were only rivalled in their handsomeness by a rainbow-coloured plumed bird found on the island, which had yard-long feathers in alternating colours and a body resembling that of an ostrich.

As if on cue, thirty young boys and girls dressed in green, like their fathers, suddenly emerged from the jungle yelling and screaming as if being pursued by the devil himself. The noise was deafening, and the bedlam distracted the parents' attention.

I briefly contemplated a possible escape while the green people's attention was diverted by the youngsters, but what was I to do? Should I make a run for it now? Would they throw more spears and fatally wound me, or tie me to a palm tree, leaving me to rot in the sun, like the skeleton of the nameless pirate we had seen on our arrival? My imagination was running wild. How would I make good my escape? Eventually, I thought better of it, realizing that I could probably not outrun the adults; I would be recaptured as soon as they turned around and noticed my absence.

I resolved to force myself to remain awake that night. While pretending to sleep, I would rack my brain to devise my plan of escape. Although they certainly treated me most kindly after they had realized that I was but a young lad, I didn't know what they had in store for me. I didn't fancy spending the rest of my life jumping around in a grass skirt being painted green every day and running through the underbrush being pursued by ferocious wildcats.

I longed for my mother and thought there was no one who would come to my rescue. Still, I refused to despair. It would be a waste of time and energy. Instead, I resolved to observe them to learn their nightly rituals and routines. Then I could perhaps make good my escape after feigning slumber or whilst helping them gather food.

I planned how then I might race to the shore, leap into the water and swim back to the ships, perhaps whilst my green captors were still asleep or otherwise preoccupied. I would attempt to make good my escape, even if I had to swim in the shark-infested waters. The natives would not easily be able to reach me with their spears, since darkness would be a perfect foil to their pursuit.

Then I wondered if the ships would even still be moored off the island. If they had already sailed, what was I to do? My fearful eyes widened and huge tears welled up, rolling down my cheeks as I gave way to uncontrollable sobbing.

The jungle people were startled by all these emotional outpourings and displays. They were taken aback by my most heartfelt sobs. How I wished I were at home with my mother at the White Horse Inn, obediently waiting on tables! That was a time when my life in the village had been most idyllic, and I thought it the most perfect place in the world.

Their kindly facial expressions and gentle touch as they solicitously ministered to my aches and pains began to put me at ease. The tallest green man, the one who had shinnied up the tree after me, and whom I had hit with the coconut, appeared to be the leader of this colourful tribe. A huge red and yellow plume protruded from his green-coiffed hair. As he gently stroked my small hand and forearm, I came to understand that he wished me no harm.

One of the other green persons, even smaller than the others, ran to the water's edge with a large strip of cork-like bark he had ripped off a lush plant with mauve orchid-like blossoms. The dwarf folded the bark a few times, then soaked it in the water until it swelled to the size of a donkey's ear, absorbing the sea water to form a spongy pad like a moist, thick bandage. He then returned and carefully applied this wet compress to the lump on my head. The plant acted as a natural poultice to bring down the swelling and dull the pain.

My eyes were wide open, riveted with wonder, though still somewhat tempered with fear. The green people's shiny black eyes were still transfixed on me, looking back at me with the same compassion and concern. Their eyes seemed to change colour with their emotional state. Caring and kindness instantaneously crosses all languages, cultural barriers and mores, translating itself in the universal language of all humanity. The natives all had little children of their own, whom they treated with the same gentleness and kindness they had shown towards me.

Meanwhile, the lads and lasses had been amusing themselves with wading into the shallow waters of the beach and observing hundreds of fantastically coloured and patterned fish of all shapes and sizes, ranging from the size of a child's baby fingernail to the size of small cats. The pure, sparkling turquoise ocean waters were teeming with fish. I observed that the natives in their hunting for food only took what they needed, thereby ensuring there would never been any shortages. They respected and revered Mother Nature as their own mothers who had given them life. Women were treated with the same high regard — a higher regard, in fact, than they received home in England.

I finally snapped out my fearful and contemplative state just as one of the jungle men began to yell loudly, gesturing excitedly in the direction of the moored ships. I was totally trapped on the island by all of these kind though fantastic-looking human beings. Their evident concern for my well-being, manifest on their faces and in their deeds, allayed my fears, at least temporarily.

Again my eyes continued to fill with tears, which rolled down my flushed cheeks at these frightening imaginings for such a young lad as myself. They had taken me into their care and confidence, but with all my aching heart I just wanted to go home. This was enough of an exotic voyage away from my secure and quiet home. I was saturated with travel, exotic or not, and with high adventure.

Just as I had become somewhat accustomed to them and comfortable in their presence — as children do with their young and impressionable minds, which are open to the world and who accept people as they are, whatever their appearance, colour or religion — my eyes were drawn towards another strange and disconcerting event.

After an unusual discourse between two of the natives — which sounded like a combination of gargling, sneezing, whistling and coughing, accompanied with pointing and an emphasis on non-English-sounding syllables — two jungle men in their mid-thirties proceeded in the direction of the jungle. They both disappeared into the luxuriant foliage, but reappeared as quickly as they had left, bearing unusual fruits and vegetables.

One variety resembled a large, rose-coloured radish about the size of an apple but with dark blue ribbons hanging from it; another looked like a gold cucumber with large purple warts on a surface mottled with blue. The food looked as exotic as the people who had gathered it.

The foods they offered were so odd and visually arresting that I was initially reluctant to try them. One of the green men laughed, then peeled one of the fruits with his sharp knife, and offered it to me. My thirst and hunger overcame my caution after my night in the palm tree, and I accepted the fruit, resolved to at least feign enjoyment in order to pacify them.

Surprisingly, I found this tropical offering sweet, juicy and pleasing to the palate as well as being thirst-quenching. The native gentleman generously offered me more when he observed my obvious enjoyment of the fruit.

As I relaxed on the beach, enjoying the odd but appetizing fruit, I saw one of the green natives clambering up a coconut tree. Suddenly, four coconuts dropped from that tree to the ground below, and I realized how badly I had misjudged the man at whom I had thrown coconuts. Climbing up a tree with a knife between their teeth was their normal means of gathering green coconuts for coconut-milk and the spoon-meat one could scrape from the inside of the unripe coconut shells. I realized that when I had thought him to be attacking me, he was merely looking for sustenance and possibly had not even noticed me at all. When I had attacked him with the coconuts, they must have taken me for some kind of wild animal who posed a threat, and had responded in kind by throwing spears.

Now knowing the circumstances — and knowing that they now knew how close they had come to accidentally killing me — I think we all experienced remorse, combined with relief that none of us had suffered permanent injury or even death.

I began to feel at ease with the natives in short order, having been treated well by them after our initial encounter in the palm tree episode. Because the green natives realized that I was just a young lad, they did not think me a threat, assuming that I lacked the strength and cunning to do anything dangerous.

I eventually came to know that these people were like anybody else or like all human beings in the world. In England, I'd had limited encounters with non-Englishmen, only meeting the occasional Scots or Irish traveller who found his way to the White Horse Inn on his way to London. At sea, however, I had met people from many, many countries. I realized that the green people were certainly no worse, and, mindful of my impressions of Ishmael Kratz, sometimes much better, than any of those I had sailed with.

Knowing now of their great kindness to me, who was a total stranger to their island, I realized that the purpose of their green colouration and plumage was likely to shock and scare potential attackers away from their isolated island, since they had no modern weaponry or defence. I knew I was safe for the time being until Captain Salisbury's crew would rescue me.

Unbeknownst to my people aboard the *Vigour*, I was in the midst of the green pygmies, wearing a grass skirt and covered with the same muddy green paint as the natives had applied to themselves. The island dwellers no doubt wanted me to draw less attention to myself by appearing to be one of them, but it would have made it harder for the captains and crews to detect me and to rescue me. Under ordinary circumstances I would not have dressed as the aboriginals did, but I had thought it best for my safety to humour them.

I soon realized, however, that other people might react to the green men as I had done and immediately assume hostile intent. If and when Captain Salisbury and his crew came to my rescue, they might attack and kill the natives, thinking that these strange-looking people were confining and mistreating me. I would have to formulate a plan to forestall retaliation against these jungle dwellers who had shown me such kindness and regard in my time of need.

I resolved to meet any potential rescuers at the water's edge and inform them that I had been well treated. I was still most apprehensive that would-be rescuers might shoot some of the jungle dwellers on sight.

I was soon brought back to reality from my musings as I found myself, along with the jungle people, surrounded by the hundred or so screeching baboon- and monkey-like creatures. Ranging in a gamut of colour from light turquoise to pastel-pink to lime-green, their huge fluffy tails could have served them as blankets at night. The beasts were jumping up and down in great excitement, creating the usual jungle mayhem and commotion, which was echoed by at least an equal number of high-pitched tropical birds, adept as they are in mimicry. The island was astir with animal activity.

"What now?" I thought to myself, unconsciously echoing the expression Captain Salisbury had more than once uttered since the commencement of our eventful sea voyage. Did these new creatures mean to do us harm? What were we to do? Could we escape from their furry clutches? What was to become of us all, this time without help from Captain Salisbury and his officers and crew and without any small boats to spirit us away?

The timbre of the noise was rising by leaps and bounds. The little native children burst out crying, ran in circles and began to create such a brouhaha that the monkeys and baboons stopped in their tracks and looked at the human children with puzzled expressions as they scratched the tops of their colourful furry heads. Perhaps they wondered to themselves how it was that these human children be noisier than their own offspring.

The adult primates placed their hands over their ears in an attempt to block out the screeching cacophony, but to no avail. The children were not in a mood to be trifled with, no matter how many monkeys and baboons surrounded them. They were thirsty, hungry, hot and tired. No primate of any description was going to get in the way of the children's next meal or even cause them any considerable discomfort. They would continue to register their displeasure, and in no uncertain terms, until the situation was rectified.

With its uncontrollable hurricanes and earthquakes, nature is the strongest force in the world. Children are the closest to nature, so they are a force to be reckoned with when displeased or denied their basic needs and rights of water, food, security and shelter. The baboons and monkeys turned heel and moved as fast as their furry feet would carry them, stampeding back to their jungle abode.

The parents were taken aback and dumbfounded by this odd behaviour and thought it might be a good tactic to employ in a future encounter with the animals, since they had never seen such creatures as these, nor any who could move so quickly. Silence once again reigned supreme; as if on cue, the birds' chatter had died away as well. I was alone on the beach, but although

I had expected to be rescued soon, no one had come ashore from the *Vigour* or the *Santa Teresita*.

I learned later that the captains and officers had agreed that the crew and passengers had earned a well-deserved lie-in the next morning, especially after having exerted themselves so much the previous day transporting people from shore to avoid the green natives and baboons. They had finally gone to bed only in the wee hours of the early morning and would be of little use in their state of exhaustion. It served no purpose to awaken them for now. They slept the sleep of the tired and the just. Certainly, no one would have had the energy to attempt my immediate rescue.

When they were finally awoken by the first officer and the midshipman, the men were instructed by the boatswain, Mr. Swanson, to check the rigging and trim the sails, along with the usual maintenance, the swabbing of decks and the general cleaning that is constantly required while shipboard. This was done after partaking of a meagre breakfast of hardtack biscuit along with boiled water. This was hardly on par with their usual fare; everyone was literally scraping the bottom of the barrel, as both ships urgently required to be completely restocked with provisions and fresh water as soon as it was safe to do so, from whatever supplies could be obtained on Blackbeard's Island.

By this point in the voyage, the biscuits were infested with weevils. Not restricting themselves to the table of the so-called lowly crew, they were equally abundant in the officers' food. The weevils' disregard for the finer distinctions of social class perhaps demonstrated at this basic level of life that the social orders are an artificial construct of man and not of nature.

10. Our ship commandeered, and fireworks

WHEN EVENING FELL, Captain Salisbury finally ordered the quartermaster to ready a longboat with a crew of ten — all the men the captains and officers could spare from their ships. This particular longboat had been used in the successful rescue of the passengers from the clutches of the enraged baboons and monkeys and still bore the long, deep scratches of their wrath along the starboard bow to prove it. The good captain was to lead the men under him in an attempt to rescue me from the completely overwhelming situation I now found myself in. All the men were well armed with musket and ball. Projecting from scabbards, their sword-hilts caught the glint of the setting sun's rays. The sailors of the landing party were anticipating a confrontation and were prepared for anything and everything.

The boat was finally lowered into the water by ropes and pulleys, with everyone on board eager to whisk me from the clutches of my captors. The boatmen plied their oars as rapidly and quietly as possible in the smooth, warm waters under the black, starry skies. Again and again they dipped their oars almost noiselessly into the calm sea, coming nearer and nearer to the shore. Salisbury was understandably worried about my present situation and was thinking about how my mother would receive the news of my untimely demise, especially as he had promised her repeatedly to look after me as if I were his own son.

A couple of lanterns were stowed in the hull of the boat, to be lit only if absolutely necessary, lest they attract undue attention to themselves, an eventuality which they wished to avoid at all cost. Lanterns would be used sparingly and with great caution, since lives were at stake. After about 35 minutes of vigorous rowing, the longboat was within a stone's throw of the sandy beach, which still retained the sun's warmth of the day. Help was on the way.

I had been left alone on the beach, still somewhat dazed and confused after all that had happened to me. Wanting to rejoin the others on ship, I had resolved to swim as speedily as I could to my seagoing home of these past two months. I hoped to avoid any man- or boy-eating sea life in the water. My fears were heightened, as I had observed some sort of creatures circling our vessel the day before. I'd had enough of beach life for the time being and knew that I would be the safest in the company of my own people and with Captain Salisbury on the *Vigour*.

Having begun wading in the shallow water and the rough-edged reefs to get to the deeper water, I spotted my would-be rescuers rowing towards the shore. I was relieved and overjoyed at seeing them. In truth, this was the happiest I had ever been to see another human being. I had imagined myself being marooned on this island until I'd be a very old man with a long beard. I was also glad that my rescuers were coming to get me, for though I fancied myself able to the task, I truly had not looked forward to the perils of a very lengthy swim.

Just as the good Captain Salisbury thought he had seen every wonder to be seen, he noticed me, his young cabin boy, in the green flesh, so to speak, as the longboat was put to shore. He leaped into the shallow water, even before the seaman was able to fully tie up the small vessel and ran towards me calling: "Christopher, Christopher! But what in God's name are you doing dressed in a grass skirt?" he blurted out in an exasperated tone. "Are you all right, lad?"

I waded quickly back towards the shore, then came to meet him, running at full speed down the beach with sand flying from my heels, and I threw my arms around him with all my might, holding on to him as if I would never let him go. He returned the hug, and I explained how I had come to be dressed as I was. This was the kind of captain we had. Only my own father could have shown me the degree of care and concern that was reflected in his kind, sympathetic and understanding face. I counted myself truly blessed that he had succeeded in reaching me.

One crewman was left to guard the longboat with a trusty set of muskets and daggers, while the remaining sailors slipped into the knee-deep water as quietly as possible, exercising caution at every turn to avoid being caught off guard. They waded quietly to the shore and then stopped, still keeping a sharp lookout, having originally intended to walk undetected to the place where Salisbury had last seen the throng of green people. That was where they had planned to go to try to rescue me, and I was grateful for their comradely concern.

Because the ships were running desperately short of water, meat and fruit, our fearless leader still had to restock the ships with provisions, despite the natives and primates remaining in full control of the island. The captain didn't know how many natives inhabited this island, so he really did not know the extent of the danger we might be in.

At this point I did not care whether I was to be rescued immediately and returned to the *Vigour* or was meant to accompany the men on their reprovisioning expedition. I was fully prepared for either eventuality, but mainly I was overjoyed to be back among Englishmen again.

The decision was made easier when all of a sudden we heard what seemed to be the roar of two hundred lions coming nearer and nearer to us. The men were on the verge of panic when the sound stopped as suddenly as it had begun. What was going on?

As Salisbury cast a glance toward the anchored ships at sea, he noticed a torch, which appeared to be suspended on the port side of the *Vigour*. How was this possible? His own night watch would be doing his rounds on the ship with a lantern. What was the explanation for this mysterious torch? Was this a deliberately set fire, or was a ghost seeking to wreak havoc on the people invading this island paradise? The torch again appeared to be floating in the air as it ascended closer within reach of the ship's railings.

Salisbury's eyes widened as they were met with the all-too-familiar sight of three green faces on his ship, their extraordinary hairdos illuminated by the flickering light of the torch's licking flames. What the devil was going on? What were they doing there, actually aboard his ship?

Salisbury in his shock and surprise (as was becoming his usual state of mind these days) was unable at first even to speak. He began to realize the full gravity of the situation. Finally he was unable to hold back his fear and apprehension, and blurted out, panic-stricken: "Oh, no! They're planning to capture the women and children on board my ship and take them hostages! They must be warned immediately!"

Still reeling from this latest setback and temporarily at a loss as to what to do, the captain unconsciously vocalized his thoughts: "What shall we do now, pray tell?" He was becoming totally overwhelmed by the whole predicament. He felt as if the whole world was conspiring against him and becoming a burden, like the unsupportable weight of the world on the mythical Atlas's shoulders. He didn't know if he could cope anymore. He had reached his breaking point.

"We must take action immediately to recapture the *Vigour,* or we are lost! We'll be marooned here for the rest of our lives!" Salisbury announced. His left shoulder was twitching in his great nervousness. The crew, captain and officers were helpless, unable to row back to their main ship in time to rescue the women and children from the clutches of the green pygmies. Who knew what schemes the indigenous people might be plotting against the unsuspecting passengers on board?

Suddenly, Salisbury caught sight of them. The fate of all the women and children, the crew and fellow officers depended upon it.

He had no time to worry about the fate of Nathaniel McCurdy, who now lay slumped on the deck. All the good captain could think about was rescuing the women and children who would soon be in the clutches of the attacking natives, and the frightening awakening they would receive on spotting the flaming torches in the pitch darkness.

Captain Salisbury had to come up with a solution or all would be lost. What were he and his officers and men to do? In the awkward situation they all now found themselves in, he consulted with his men to devise a plan on the spot.

The captain and his men decided to scatter across the beach to alert the sleeping people on the ship to the impending danger by firing warning shots into the air. I joined the other sailors in banging together the overturned copper pots and iron pans that had been left behind when they had fled the beach in the three longboats. The din could have raised the dead.

The unsuspecting people aboard the *Vigour* had no time to lose. Captain Salisbury did not know if the ship's crew and the guest passengers from the *Santa Teresita* would awaken in time to raise a defence against the diminutive interlopers, but he knew that we had done what we could. He made a mental note that if they got out of this latest scrape alive, he would require the rope ladders on their ships to be taken up every night so that no foe could ever again board their vessels unbeknownst to themselves, thereby compromising the security of the whole ship — and of her women and children, especially.

"This is all we can do to help them at present. The natives have totally commandeered my ship!" exclaimed the horrified Salisbury. His men were ashen; shock was etched on their faces.

The green natives on the *Vigour*, now numbering about 70, were pouring into the hold at great speed from the quarterdeck. They had lit ten more torches that had been stored in a metal trunk against the mizzenmast. As the captors disappeared below deck, he could only see four green people left on the main deck guarding the ship to stop any would-be rescuers from boarding their newly captured prize.

The captain was apprehensive that the natives would torch his ship if he attempted to rescue his charges with the aid of the remaining crew, but under the cover of darkness, the numerous clouds engulfing the full moon would provide perfect conditions for an attempted rescue of the captured women and children on the *Vigour*.

The screams of the shipboard women and children who at that moment had been rudely awakened from their restful sleep were now heard, echoing loudly on the beach. The men were distraught, but all became too stunned, unsettled and distressed to react in their defence.

Through his spyglass Salisbury saw the womenfolk and children being herded onto the top deck of the ship, still in nightclothes, all the while being threatened with sharp bamboo spears held dangerously close to their throats and chests.

Captain Salisbury ordered us all to board the longboat without wasting time, as people's lives and limbs were once more in imminent danger. We leapt into our waiting boat as fast as was humanly possible, and the men began to row briskly.

The green people, speaking amongst themselves in their own language, were, unbeknownst to Salisbury and the other captains, hatching a plot of their own, intended to rid their island paradise of us all, whom they perceived as unwelcome, over-bearing and demanding occupiers. What were they to do, being outnumbered and without the superior muskets and flintlocks which could inflict fatal casualties? The chief of the group had observed the casks of gunpowder which had been stored amid-ships. He had noticed with curiosity that some of the powder had spilled on the deck when their group had commandeered the *Vigour*. When inadvertently some flaming coconut oil fell from his torch onto the black unknown substance, it had begun to spark and flame like fireworks. Luckily, there was only a small amount of the gunpowder on the floor.

Fascinated by this effect, he discussed his discovery with the rest of the tribe, thinking that this would be an excellent diversionary tactic to help them make good their escape. Just think of what effects could be achieved with a barrel or two of this unknown mixture, he told his follower. A group of them took coconut oil, mixed it with the gunpowder and applied the mixture to their grass skirts. If things got difficult, they could whip off the skirts and set fire to them to create a distraction.

When we were midway to the *Vigour*, I noticed a trickle of water entering the hull of the boat where I was seated. I informed the Captain immediately of this. In the choppy water we had rowed the boat too close to a reef. The hull had struck a sharp rock outcrop, which had slightly damaged the boat. As the boat was taking on water, we needed either to bail or to repair it.

I thought quickly and kneaded some of the boiled sticky sap from unripe breadfruits, a kind of chewy substance that the pygmies had given to me to keep my compress from slipping off my head. It had remained on my forehead, and I no longer needed it. I placed the kneaded resinous gum in the hole to fill the leak, and it seemed to do the trick. It would hold temporarily, at least until the ship's carpenter could do a proper repair.

The natives still seemed fascinated by the fair-skinned women and children, who were perhaps as exotic to them as the green pygmies were to all of us. They examined with their tiny childlike hands the varying colours of the young children's hair, especially the coppery hair of the girl triplets, whose ample ringlets bounced as they moved. Their locks looked like soft copper tubes. Curiosity overcame them, as it oftentimes does when one is confronted with novelty and newness of experience. It is a basic human trait not exercised often enough.

The children, in the main, also found the native strangers equally as interesting and engaging, since these youngsters' encounters with the New World and its inhabitants had been limited to this first sea voyage in their young lives. They were quite intrigued by their small hands, and compared them to the size of their own. They were not fearful of the green people, but eyed them with curiosity.

"Mother?" asked one quizzical five-year-old with a serious look on her face, "why does this little green man keep looking at my hair? Hasn't he seen any hair before?"

"Maybe he is interested in it because it's different from most people's. It's a novelty, my dearest," was her mother's reasonable answer.

"Mother?" the child asked again thoughtfully and after more deliberation, having watched a young native's hair bobbing about in the moonlight. "Why does he wear his hair just the same way my dolly does?" Her mother, at a loss as to what to say, left the question unanswered, her head shaking almost imperceptibly back and forth to register her lack of knowledge on the subject.

The green invaders started to examine the wide array of hair colours, liberally applying their agile little hands to study their captives' heads. The women's and children's hair ranged from carrot-red to the fairest flaxen yellow. The women were quite taken aback by the liberties these unknown individuals were taking, and they registered displeasure by pulling the children's heads away from the green pygmies' little groping hands.

The ladies were shocked at the apparent immodesty of the grass skirts the natives wore in the presence of themselves and their equally innocent children. They protested this vulgarity by covering their children's eyes with their shaking hands and averting their own.

The youngest children, on the other hand, registered and reflected the fear of their parents, but were more intrigued than ever by these unusual-looking individuals and viewed them with temerity from between their parents' fingers. They began to giggle as they observed the natives' green colouration and grass skirts. Some of the natives began smiling widely at the young children, reflecting their good humour. Some of the youngest toddlers shocked their mothers by suggesting that they wanted to wear the very same costumes.

"Mummy," asked an innocent lad not much more than four years old, "can we dress like that sometime at our next costume party? It looks like good fun!"

"I should say not, Chesworth! What would your father think?" was the mother's curt reply.

The green "pirates" were at a loss, unsure of how to deal with so many women and children. Some of the 30-odd youngsters were running up to them, trying to flip up their grass skirts, pinching them, sticking out their tongues and thumbing their noses. After engaging in this new-found "sport," they would run back to their mothers or governesses and exclaim with glee, while exhibiting no demonstrable fear of their captors anymore. The ensuing pandemonium soon involved all the children, ranging in age from two-month-old babies to the 14-year-olds.

Children naturally react in the private world of their youthful counterparts before they engage themselves in the emotions of the adult world. Children have an inherent rapport with each other that defies all colour, nationality or religion in the human race. They are at one with each other and inherently possess this quality until they enter into the mysterious realms of adulthood. A child is a child, wherever on earth he or she is, and each is made from the same mould of humanity, no matter what colour he or she is.

Meanwhile, the cacophony of the young ones was becoming unbearable for all the adults — those sporting coats of green mud and those without. This noise was beginning to unnerve the invaders, who were virtually outnumbered, so much so that they clapped their hands over their ears to avoid the incessant din of the clambering children, then turned tail and ran, finally leaping off the closest deck into the water. The green privateers had been driven to distraction by their noise and constant activity and were seeking an escape at any cost. They were totally accustomed to the peace and quiet of nature and of their own children, who reflected this characteristic.

The green people fortunately missed hitting the logs which they had hastily and loosely lashed together to paddle out on, and which now were tied by sisal rope to the lee side of the bow of the *Vigour*.

Storm clouds had gathered, rapidly darkening the skies as thunder and lightning began to fill the heavens. The ensuing winds rose to gale force and now started to ravage the 60 or more palm trees lining the beach, almost ripping some of them out of the sand by their roots. The swirling winds started to snap the tops off the most vulnerable of the trees.

Palm fronds resembled spinning tops as they flew through the air, some of them barely missing the green men returning to the beach. The thunder was deafening and echoed across the island; each lightning bolt lit up the skies with what seemed to be a million candlepower. It sounded much like the fireworks over Hampton Court in London on Guy Fawkes Day as the fork lightning lit up the dark skies again and again, frightening the women and children on deck, who now felt the threat of being struck by the constant display of nature's fury.

One of the natives had been struck on his bottom with a lightning bolt, much to the surprise of their former captives. His grass skirt burst into flames in mid-air. He was then tossed up into the air by a gust of wind, which threw him against the mizzenmast before another updraft flipped him into the water, his skirt still alight, where he landed with a sizzling sound, a small plume of steam arising where the fire was extinguished. All that could be seen of the unfortunate victim's face was his exceptionally white eyeballs and teeth that seemed almost to glow in the dark, and his skin took on an eerie, ghostly glow.

Three other escapees' skirts also burst into flames in rapid succession after they leapt over the mid-ship deck. They had all become part of the human fireworks show, much to their own dismay and discomfort, as was reflected on their contorted and shocked faces. Being struck by lightning bolts had triggered these odd chemical reactions on their painted skin. They were still glowing with their ghostly green shapes in the dark as they escaped, swimming towards the beach as fast as they could.

The women and children on board watched these events with shock, not knowing what to anticipate next and staring at the guardrails of the ship, where some of the green men had seemingly burst into flame before their very eyes. Later it was a wonder to us that none of our intruders had suffered very serious injuries or even death.

When they reached shore after wildly paddling their make-shift logs or swimming, they sprinted as fast as their little green, glowing feet would carry them into the thick jungle underbrush, some of them stumbling on the way.

After the women and children on board the *Vigour* had witnessed the last native disappearing into the night, they all attempted to return to their previous sleeping arrangements, while the guards — whom the green natives had previously attacked — roused from their unconscious state and were given medical treatment. The broad-shouldered, muscled guards had only sustained minor injuries.

Four of the tallest and most sturdily built women filled out the night watch so that any more unwelcome night-time intruders would be soundly repelled should they suddenly appear out of nowhere.

11. Safe return aboard the *Vigour*

In about twenty-five minutes, we arrived at our ship, the *Vigour*, safe and dry, with the long boat in no immediate danger of sinking. Reaching the port side, we all clambered up the rope ladder, carefully picking our way as usual. I was so happy to be back on the ship surrounded by my shipmates and Captain Salisbury, my saviour and benefactor.

I breathed easier once on board. Despite the departure of the green invaders, pandemonium still prevailed. In the *mêlée*, some young children had become separated from their mothers and nannies. A toddler not more than three years old was screaming loudly. I took the frightened lad by the hand and told him to be quiet. I tried to reason with the lad but soon found it was to no avail. He soon burst into tears again and started screaming hysterically, beside himself with fear. I was at my wits' end by this time.

"Be quiet! Come with me! We'll find your mother!" I said sharply, trying to drown out his crying. I was, at first, utterly ineffective at calming him.

"We must look everywhere — on all decks! Follow me!" I commanded. The toddler followed me obediently, beginning to sense my good intentions, I hoped. Truth be told, the poor little creature would probably have gone with anyone who displayed a shred of human kindness. We looked on the main deck for his nanny and mother, but there would be so much shrieking, hysteria and emotional outpourings at seeing another supposed green native that I thought it best to hide out until things had settled down on the ship.

I finally hustled the toddler below deck into the ship's galley. I looked around hastily before opening the door to the carpenter's cabin to the left of the galley stove, then quickly pulled the toddler into the room as quietly as possible to avoid attracting undue attention.

Someone might well have misconstrued the situation we were in. With the green paint not having washed off and with me still wearing my grass skirt, they might easily have thought that I was one of the original green people, intent on doing harm to the young lad. I locked and secured the carpenter's cabin door from the inside. We were safe for the time being.

After what seemed to be an eternity, the screaming of the women and children subsided as calm returned to the ship. We could hear the sound of someone frantically calling out a name.

"Thomas, Thomas! Where are you, child?" implored a frantic voice near the carpenter's door.

"Mummy, mummy! I'm in here!" replied the child, with obvious relief and happiness in his shining eyes. Taken aback by this surprising turn of events, I fumbled to open the cabin door. As the door was flung aside, the toddler raced out as fast as his little legs would carry him into the waiting arms of his raven-haired mother. Tears shone on her cheeks at the sight of her lost son as she scooped him into her arms.

"Thomas, my love!" she sobbed. "I thought they had taken you from me and that I would never see you again, my love." She sobbed with happiness as she hugged him again and again. It is really only under the direst circumstances that parents realize the depth and extent of their love and attachment for their children, who are indeed their greatest jewels and treasures of the world. Neither diamonds nor treasure chests full of pieces of eight can substitute for a mother's or parent's love for their offspring.

I smiled happily while witnessing this touching, tearful and heartfelt reunion of mother and child. The mother, after regaining her composure, looked at me in a most disconcerted way. Her consternation made me most self-conscious, and I was suddenly reminded of my physical appearance, with my long grass skirt and green-tinged skin. What was I to do? Regaining my own composure, I tried to calm her by addressing her directly:

"Excuse me, ma'am. Are you and your son quite all right?"

The young woman was startled to realize that I spoke English. She was immediately struck by the oddness of the situation with a young lad like myself dressed in native attire, speaking to her with a proper English accent. She was totally taken aback and had misgivings with regard to her safety and that of her child.

"You aren't going to harm us, are you?" she asked timorously.

"No, ma'am," was my pure and simple answer.

"I say," she said screwing up her courage to talk to me once more. "How is it that you speak English? This is highly irregular, I must say!"

"I'm Christopher Berkshire, the cabin boy from the *Vigour*," I explained.

"I was captured by the green natives who gave me this dreadful grass skirt."

"Of course. I recognize you now. You're the cabin boy who brought me the colic water for Thomas and the anise-ginger tea three days ago," the young lady said, with noticeable relief in her voice.

The words spilled out faster and faster as I began to relate my story of heart-stopping adventure and excitement to the young woman, who gave me her undivided attention. This had been the first opportunity I'd had to speak in my own language since my capture. I finally felt free to express the pent-up feelings and fears of my tender young heart and mind.

The young mother was astonished by my story, her eyes widening with every word I uttered. The child was also transfixed and was responding to my timbre of voice and gesticulations, imitating his mother's expressions.

Children often reflect and naturally imitate the emotional state of their parents and other adults, gradually absorbing what society expects of them and internalising the unspoken rules for behaviour and social interaction. Every culture in the world is similar, differing only in a greater or lesser degree. People are much the same the world over, since they all belong to one human race. The variations are slight, being that of skin colour and differing ideas. We are all one family that believe in family.

Later, after I'd had an opportunity to change into my usual seafaring clothing, Captain Salisbury told me that he had been worried about me but had been preoccupied by the matters at hand, including the welfare of the other crew and passengers on both ships. He intimated that he had every confidence in my ingenuity, resourcefulness and self-reliance, and that he had in any case made a decision to intervene later the next day to try to rescue me, since nothing else could be done about the situation while he still had direct responsibility for the people they had rescued in the longboats.

The captain had hoped I would remain undetected where I had hidden in the tree and that, if captured, I would be treated with gentleness — especially as I was only twelve and would not seem overtly threatening. He had been clearly distressed about my situation but could do nothing about it at the time. Events were unfolding as they should and would not be thwarted by the likes of the hairy beasts and the green people on the island.

Now Salisbury, too, wished to be home and far away from these foreign climes. Life was racing out of control for him once again. One is only able to gain a perspective on the situation when one can distance oneself from events with a change of scenery and rational thinking.

Meanwhile, the young baker, Simon Crudgely, stared intently out to sea on the main deck, having also been caught up in the events. He also reflected on his own sea journey over the last two months, of shipwreck, marooning and harrowing escape by raft, and of his rescue by our able crew. He sorely missed family life to the very core of his young existence and longed to see his mother, father and new baby sister after his short time at sea. He missed the safety, security and familiarity of his small village, with the delicious smells of baking bread and buns wafting through the air down the cobblestoned streets from his father's bakery and throughout the village. Such pleasant domestic thoughts now occupied his mind. No doubt he still could appreciate the excitement and adventure that sea life afforded, but there were limits to what the human mind could take in. Eventually it must return to the familiarity of its past, simple stable life, even if only for a short while, to once again regain a balance in life, mind and body.

As for me, I soon fell into my berth, relieved and exhausted by the day's turn of events. I felt sure that we would soon set sail for our next destination to avoid the wrath of the primates and perhaps that of the green natives. Salisbury was not a man to take chances with the lives of his passengers and crew.

The women and children on deck had thought that they had seen the last of the green people, but then noticed two more seated on a large log, paddling frantically with broken pieces of wooden flotsam and jetsam nearing the beach where the others had abandoned their logs minutes before.

Before reaching dry land, however, the palm-tree trunk on which they had been escaping was struck by another lightning bolt and shattered as they leapt off it. Some of the wooden debris rained down on the heads of the unfortunate victims, knocking them headlong into the water again.

After their accidental baptism, they splashed their way to shore and then sprinted off into the thick foliage as fast as their little, thin green legs would carry them, much to the relief of the women and children on the ship who had been watching.

On the beach, Alvarez, standing next to his crew members, had observed with our most recent incident that 70 or so green natives had originally taken over the *Vigour* and had been standing on the deck of the ship shaking their spears at the fear-struck passengers and crew members. But only 40 had leapt off the decks in their bid to escape from their tormentors. Alvarez wondered where the other 30 or so aboriginal people might be hiding. They couldn't be accounted for.

Meanwhile, back on the *Vigour,* just when he thought that things couldn't possibly get worse, Salisbury heard the now familiar sound of women and children screaming from the mid-ship deck. He scrambled up the steps from his cabin, only to observe, to his astonishment, ten women and children in their night clothing being chased in circles on the main deck by five or six screeching and wild-eyed, deranged, mauve- and pink-striped apes, one of which was flicking a cat-o'-nine tails at the bottoms of the screaming, fleeing humans.

And where were the other 30 or so other green natives who were no longer to be seen? Were they going to leap out of the shadows at him and fellow officers and captains? Salisbury's anxiety increased at the thought of this great unknown. What else could possibly occur at this point in time? His mouth became dry, his chest tightened and a lump arose in his throat as heightened foreboding gripped him. An overwhelming sensation of panic overtook him and his breath was stifled and choking in his chest. All of a sudden, Captain Salisbury and the others found themselves surrounded by the hitherto missing green people. The ferocious, glistening-faced island people menacingly pointed their long bamboo spears at their captives' gulping throats.

Just as quickly as they had appeared, the natives suddenly disappeared when they saw the mayhem of the apes with their threatening antics. They jumped off the lee side of the ship with the apes in hot pursuit, as if wishing them a less-than-fond farewell and speed them on their way. They began to swim more furiously than ever to shore after their green bodies hit the water — indeed, as fast as their little arms and legs could carry them.

All the while, the captain and officers had been distracted by the antics of the pastel apes and colourful baboons on deck. These green people had previously concealed wood torches soaked in coconut oil in a nearby cave in the jungle not far from the beach where we now found ourselves. The natives had put themselves out of harm's way until their counterparts returned from the *Vigour*.

How could Alvarez and Salisbury defend themselves from such unpredictable and unwelcome company? For the life of him, Salisbury could not come up with a plan to escape. Having been caught off guard, the would-be rescuers had become temporary captives themselves.

The green people then herded us into a small circle on the beach, all the while pointing and shaking their weapons at us threateningly. All the men had been tied together with a long sisal rope. The good captain had just about reached the point where if he wasn't experiencing some emergency situation with excessive amounts of adrenalin coursing through his veins, he no longer felt his normal self.

The two captains would have to make good their escape if they were to aid the distressed women and children, who were still being pursued by the huge, lumbering apes. The Spanish captain and Salisbury mulled various possibilities and finally devised a plan for escape.

The two agreed that they would wait until the natives had turned in for the night and then would attempt to free themselves by overpowering their captors. The men were unable to sleep well anyway, being bound up in such an uncomfortable and confining way. Later, when the green people fell asleep, the captives helped each other to become free from their sisal bonds, then slipped away from their snoring captors, thus escaping in the middle of the night.

The majority of the freed men paddled out to the *Vigour* by leaping onto the remaining logs so that the jungle people could not readily follow them. The rest of the escapees swam speedily to the awaiting ship. Salisbury was glad he had once insisted that all his men learn to swim properly. Many sailors had been swept overboard in his time, and some had drowned from not knowing this basic survival skill. They stealthily boarded their own vessel by scrambling up the ropes and concealed themselves in the shadows of their ship so as not to be detected by the apes now sleeping all over the main deck, apparently preferring the cool night air to the stifling heat of the cabins below deck where the women and children had been confined.

The captain and his men used tinderboxes to light twenty torches, and each man stood hovering over the sleeping apes. The snoring primates were now rudely awakened. They were terrified at the flames before their faces and started screeching in horror. They leapt to their feet in a panic, trembling from head to toe. If these unfortunate creatures had not already caused everyone so much undue trouble and commotion, Salisbury would have felt genuinely sorry for their plight. As it was, the captains and crew drove them off the ship in short order, prodding and threatening them with the torch-flames licking their quivering backsides. It was too close for comfort for the animals as they leapt off the ship to find welcome relief in the ocean below. They swam back to shore going as fast as their large, hairy arms and legs would carry them.

After the many days of turmoil, silence and peace reigned supreme on the *Vigour*, with the women and children once again safe and sound. Eight guards, six more than on the usual watch, were posted on deck to protect everyone on board from the potential return of natives, apes or chimpanzees who might still be lurking in the jungles hatching another plan of attack.

The Spanish captain later determined that the greenish people had paddled out to the *Vigour* one hour before under the cover of darkness and lay in wait on the windward side of the ship until the commanders and crew departed for the island, knowing full well that they were going to try to rescue me.

After their usual breakfast repast, Captains Salisbury and Alvarez returned with their handpicked crew the same day to the island to determine the state of the natives whom they had been left sleeping. They found remnants of fermented fruit, mostly persimmons, jackfruit, and pineapples, littering the jungle floor where they had first encountered the angered primates in the previous evening's foray.

The clever primates would habitually throw chopped-up or half-eaten fruit into wooden barrels near their cave where they had first encountered humans. These barrels were partially filled with navy rum and had evidently been abandoned or washed ashore from a previous shipwreck or landing.

Markings on the side of the barrels indicated that they had contained over-proof spirits originating from the Royal Navy. The original spirits may have been left either by marauding pirate bands, by a landing party of English sailors who had previously arrived on this isolated island to take on fresh provisions and supplies, or by someone marooned on the island some years ago. Obviously, this was pure speculation, since no witnesses remained to relate the series of events which led to their drunkenness. Only the island and its ghosts of the past knew the truth of what had transpired during these mysterious times.

Salisbury learned that as little as a quarter cup of the animals' liquor-soaked fermenting fruit mixture would suffice to drive these normally well-behaved primates into a world of unpredictable behaviour, staggering about the tropical island in a state of drunkenness. When the primates had boarded his ship in the middle of the night, they had understandably been in an agitated state, burdened as they were with very delicate and sensitive constitutions, much like humans in the first decade of their lives, and were in no mood to be toyed with or provoked in their drunken state.

Unbeknownst to the captain, one of his men had sampled the potent brew and soon began demonstrating the same belligerent behaviour, most undesirable in an honest, sober seaman. Salisbury had a hard time stopping the other men from imitating his example, and he ordered them, in no uncertain terms, to cease from consuming this potent mixture. He didn't need another incident to add to his already nearly endless list of dangerous misadventures as he sought refuge and peace from his tumultuous high-seas life.

Just as he was about to complete his thought, about a hundred apes and chimpanzees of the varying colours of the rainbow and all combinations in the pastel world, burst out of the jungle and began pursing the good captain and his landing party. "What in the devil is going on now?" Salisbury wondered as he and his men sprinted towards the jungle with the lurching apes and chimpanzees in hot pursuit. The primates' legs were wobbling as they staggered drunkenly towards the sailors, officers and captains, showing their sharp teeth and claws.

When the chimpanzees and apes had finally recovered from the effects of the alcoholic binge, they had been left in the dust by the humans, who thought they were still being pursued by the angry primates. After reaching the longboat, Salisbury and Alvarez ordered their crews to row quick-time. The English captain, being a reflective personality, for a brief moment noted this odd and inconsistent behaviour of the primates. Was it not odd and puzzling how the animals, which had treated them all so considerately and been so generous in the beginning, offering food to generously help and sustain their human counterparts, virtually saving their lives, could now, under the effects of alcohol, behave so badly towards the selfsame people they had earlier saved? Inconsistent and violent in their behaviour, they could not easily be dealt with during their drunken outbursts of ranting and raving, but only after the effects of the alcohol had worn off. Hopefully this would occur sooner than later, Captain Salisbury thought to himself.

The noise of the screaming and stampeding men reached the ears of the sleeping green people. They bolted upright in the spots where they had fallen asleep. They were disconcerted and confused to find themselves once again in the thick of things with enraged primates staggering around the beaches falling into the red and yellow hibiscus bushes and coming out again with the tropical flowers hanging out of their ears and nostrils, all the while screeching and lunging at each other as if in a drunken primate dance. Bristling at the thought of another encounter with their beastly counterparts, the green men pointed in their direction and uttered grunting, whistling, and yodelling sounds. The beasts seemed to respond in kind as they walked up to them sedately. They had been pacified by the little green gentlemen in their natural behaviour, being the closest of all human beings to nature.

The green men knew how to handle the fickle primates, since they had all grown up in the same environment and had encountered them before. These huge baboons and monkeys were considered much like house pets, with the intelligence of young children. They were also employed to gather food, to clean the huts and generally to assist the native women in their chores of making clothing and doing domestic work as required, like unpaid servants.

12. More monkeyshines

ABOUT TWO HOURS LATER INTO NIGHT, shrieks and screams of terror arose from the men sleeping in their hammocks. "Help, help! We're being attacked! Help! Salisbury and Alvarez awoke and leapt to their feet.

"What's happening here? What the devil is going on here?" demanded Salisbury, with consternation in his voice, whipping his head around in the direction of the shrieking men.

Many had been rudely awakened by flying baboons and monkeys who wished to experience lying in the hammocks themselves; they leaped out of trees and bounced onto the hammocks like trampolines. They performed impressive feats of derring-do, jumping from considerable heights, rolling the shrieking and terrified sailors out of the hammocks they had been occupying and onto the damp jungle floor. A few landed in small puddles of jungle water after being thrown out of their swinging beds, having been so rudely awakened by the energetic primates. Some fully-clothed men landed on their *derrières*, splashing themselves with muddy water up to their eyeballs and beyond, seemingly to the great delight of the apes, which seemed to laugh, pointing their fingers at the humans' folly. Pandemonium ensued as the humans ran, in fear of being physically attacked again by the large jungle animals which could easily have flattened any of the men in their vicinity.

Then, other beasts of all natures and colours came charging out of the jungle and descended upon the hapless sailors, pursuing the unfortunate cowering and shaking ones who had not already been tossed from their hammocks slung between the trees.

All the while, great primate screams were heard, and the put-upon humans screamed and shrieked in their turn. They were seized with terror, running every which way, willy-nilly, to escape from their rainbow-coloured, hairy attackers. Some sought refuge up trees, while others made for the ocean and attempted to outswim their pursuers to the anchored ship.

Everyone else by this time was awoken by all these violent outbursts, except for one nearly deaf old salt who managed to sleep, murmuring indecipherable words and phrases throughout it all, smiling to himself.

The women and children on the ships awoke, startled by the loud shrieking and screaming, when they saw that enraged primates were chasing the menfolk. The monkeys' jaws opened wide as they gnashed their teeth, exposing their huge yellow fangs and drooling gums.

The children, who had been sleeping on deck, burst out crying at seeing their parents and adults being pursued in such a dangerous and unprovoked manner; the rude awaking struck terror into their little hearts.

"Papa, papa!" a little girl with blonde ringlets shrieked.

"Look out behind you!" Her high-pitched voice easily carried over the confusion. A large baboon with brilliant purple eyes set deep in his sockets was pursuing two unfortunate men at top speed. Ten other hairy creatures sprinted after the panicking humans.

Wide-eyed and frantic, one men was barely able to avoid the snapping jaws of an enraged beast. The other gentleman threw the beast off his trail, jumping fully clothed into the ocean; the terrified child's father followed suit.

Both men then swam vigorously towards their ship, when several dolphins leaped into the air in unison. As they landed on their sides, they produced great splashes of water, which soaked the threatening primates. The sea creatures had come to the rescue of the humans, and the awed men could scarcely believe their good fortune at having being rescued by these intelligent animals. As quickly as they appeared, the dolphins then swam away, to be seen no more.

The soaked baboons turned heel and lumbered back to the jungle as fast as their huge, hairy feet would carry them. The sheer volume of their loud protestations rendered the people of the island temporarily deaf.

At least some of the baboons, monkeys and apes seemed to have an aversion to water — save for drinking it, of course. Water regularly poured off the huge leaves of the rubber trees like spouts and could be found in the jungle after heavy downpours and be drunk as needed. Some of the primates stood under a particular leaf with their mouths open, slaking their thirsts in the oppressive equatorial heat. A few of them, however, would occasionally engage in a quick shower, which they seemed to delight in, with the female monkeys sometimes holding their struggling babies underneath the cooling waters.

Birds of every colour, size and description ranging from bright purples, oranges and pink to magenta and marigold and every other combinations thereof filled the sky, in an attempt to flee the loud ranting of both man and beast. It was a tropical rainbow of colour in what appeared to be the garden of Eden.

Captain Salisbury, his officers and the passengers under his command had never seen such abundance, variety and diversity of tropical coloured fowl or beast in all their previous travels. Teeming in the tropical waters off the island were also fish of every description and colour, from pure gold to silvery purples, bright oranges and reds and every other colour in between and combinations thereof. Truly, they put the rainbow to shame. The sheer variety of these underwater creatures fascinated and delighted the most jaundiced and worldly person on the voyage.

The rudely awakened sailors looked with awe and wonder at the schools of fish, which varied in size from fingerlings to ten stone or more. The fish had likely never encountered human beings before, since they showed a distinct lack of fear or concern at their presence. It was later observed that the smaller fish showed a marked preference for children, as they would sometimes swim in circles around some of the wee ones in the shallower waters.

The children giggled and shrieked with delight at the sight at these new-found wonders of nature. The fish would gently caress and delicately brush against them with their long, trailing tails and fins, tickling the children in the water, to their utmost delight. A school of a hundred dazzling silver and turquoise fish once swam towards the other men, women and children who had entered water to bathe or cool off from the oppressive heat. The women were modestly and fastidiously attired for bathing in the fashion of the day, covered nearly head to foot with their gauzy costumes.

Dr. Loyster had not yet determined what fish were edible, or even identified the various species. Some were completely new to him. He was eager to proceed with a study, and his talented illustrator, Edouard Lepine, was equally impatient to execute his illustrations. He, too, had never before encountered such an abundance and variety of fish in his travels, and he planned eventually to present his findings to the Royal Society upon his return to London. The sheer volume and abundance of fowl and fish was overwhelming. It would likely have taken the naturalist and illustrator many months or even years of hard work to study, illustrate and catalogue the flora and fauna on this teeming and abundant tropical paradise. The plethora of new plants and animals was mind-boggling. It was truly an ideal tropical paradise.

Suddenly an enormous flock of beautifully coloured birds filled the sky, making sounds of evident alarm and flying in all directions, as if they were attempting to escape from a predator. What was causing them to behave in such a manner? They had in fact been startled by the violent movements of the humans being thrown to the ground out of their hammocks and by the erratic and uncharacteristic behaviour of the monkeys and baboons.

Dr. Loyster later came to learn that the area the men had chosen to sleep in was one which had been regularly frequented by the monkeys and baboons on their daily hunting and food gathering expeditions. The unaccustomed presence of the men had understandably upset the primates on their daily search for food; they saw the humans as invaders to their prosperous island. Their usual routine had been totally disrupted by both the passengers and crew alike.

The primates soon settled down, and their screeching subsided, with order restored on the island for both man and beast, as baboon and monkey babies were reunited with their concerned parents. Everyone was living in harmony for the time being, and calm was restored to the island home. Most of the people had been fatigued from their vigorous activities of the day before. They had all been lulled into a state of oblivion by their dreams. The people on the ships were also finally able to enjoy a good night's sleep.

13. We run aground

EANWHILE, ON THE OTHER SIDE of the island, some of the green people who were now rousing and rising to their feet were unaware of what had transpired. Green and orange paint was dripping down their faces after a tropical downpour had erupted. They were also hungry and tired from their previous night's high-flying performances off the *Vigour*. They came over to where the sailors had spent the night ashore, and were pointing to their mouths and rubbing their stomachs as the bystanders observed them with a mixture of fear and measured curiosity.

The blood-red grass skirts of the natives were becoming soaked in the torrential downpour and were by now infusing the sand with colour. They were starting to resemble not so much pre-historic flying lizards as drowned cockroaches in their wet raffia skirts. Rain poured in torrents from the heavens and showed no signs of abating. Then, just as suddenly as the downfall had begun, it stopped abruptly. The sun broke through the clouds, the skies were azure, and the tropical waters once again assumed a turquoise brilliance, with green and purple parrots filling the air with loud birdcalls.

Captain Salisbury, however, woke early so that he could have a report from the sentries on duty who had been posted around their makeshift camp. They had been on night watch and were patrolling their area on the beach and in the jungle to make certain that the group was not attacked during the night by the same or different wild beasts; they could not risk being taken unawares. One had to be alert to dangers at all times. Salisbury decided to wake Alvarez so that he could consult with him on what to do.

Alvarez and Salisbury had to consider what they were going to do with these new creatures and what they were all going to eat. He had enough trouble already, just feeding his own lot. What were Salisbury and Alvarez to do with them? It proved to be a problem of logistics, supply and demand. They would likely have to ration food until they could establish a definite, abundant and reliable supply.

Would they leave them confined on the same island until the ships and passengers were safe sailing off to home? At an impromptu meeting the captains and officers decided to forcibly confine the green people on the *Santa Teresita* and transport them to La Graciosa, a small, uninhabited island less than five nautical miles south. With similar vegetation and animal life, but without boats, they would not pose any more danger to us as the newest temporary inhabitants of their new home. They would be returned to their original island paradise only after the galley and larders had been restocked with fresh fruit, game and water, along with breadfruit and spices.

This was to be done at the crack of dawn to ensure there was time for the prisoners to travel to the island during daylight hours and for them to hunt for food and water.

The natives were stunned at their unceremonious expulsion from their own home. Who were these foreigners to forcibly uproot them from their own island? They had lived here for untold generations in contentment and in harmony with nature. The aboriginal people were talking amongst themselves in their melodious native language. Although the guards, ten of Alvarez's crewmen, did not understand this language, they observed the kidnapped aboriginal people becoming more and more agitated as their voices rose to a fever pitch in the balmy morning air. They hadn't partaken of food or water for eight hours or more, so they were not in a mood to be trifled with. Though justifiable resentment was mounting amongst the wronged green men, they were forced aboard the Spanish ship and confined there at the points of swords and muskets. This was adding insult to injury!

Alvarez sailed south to the lee side of La Graciosa. The green men had been given wooden buckets filled with clean drinking water as they huddled together on the main deck. They slaked their thirst with the precious liquid, which they extracted by means of a small metal dipper. The resentment on their faces was growing by the minute and was becoming more pronounced as they furtively eyed their captors and enemies. If looks could truly kill, there would have been piles of seamen's corpses lying about the decks. The aboriginal people were becoming more and more agitated as they neared the island. Their discontent became pronounced and more heated as Captain Alvarez anchored the ship near the uninhabited island.

As the natives surveyed the new island, they were astounded to see numerous strange limestone configurations, which had been eroded by extreme winds and torrential rainfalls to produce the effect of giant freestanding finger-like sculptures.

"My word!" murmured Salisbury, in his astonishment at seeing this surrealistic landscape. It was as if he had mistakenly happened upon a different planet since sailing from the previous island.

Captain Alvarez stood next to him with an equally stunned expression, quietly crossing himself. Even the most seasoned and hardened of the men stood in silent amazement at this new and startling landscape.

Meanwhile, the natives continued to point their fingers accusingly at their captors while angrily exchanging glances. Their discontented muttering grew louder, and they were now glaring at the crew and officers. Captain Salisbury observed the prisoners with growing fear, his mind flashing back to how Kratz had attempted to incite his crewmen to mutiny. The natives were no doubt planning a reprisal for the actions of these white devils. Their intense defiant and threatening looks were distressing to behold. Salisbury, as usual, would have to nip this in the bud. Fortunately, curiosity about their new surroundings temporarily distracted the prisoners, and their eyes registered the same mix of fear, fascination and incredulity as everyone else.

This was something they had not seen before and could not possibly have imagined. A strange and foreboding landscape, with fantastic, swirled columns of rock like hundred-foot chimney pots glittered in hues of purple and pink across the landscape. The marbled stone seemed covered in diamonds and amethysts sparkling and glittering in the bright rays of the sun. The captains, officers and crew alike felt as if they had been transported to a fantasy world. Apprehension registered on their faces at the bizarre beauty thrust before their eyes.

Fear can all too easily set into the human psyche when a change of environment is too great for the mind to bear, due to its direct contrast to familiar reality. The mind can tolerate some change but not a 360-degree turnabout. What were Salisbury, Alvarez and their small crews to do? It would be not merely uncharitable but inhumane to drop these green people into this alien place without food or water. They would be morally amiss to do so. "What to do? What to do?" he thought to himself. As Captain Salisbury was contemplating his moral dilemma, he spotted a zebra-like creature with green and white stripes and a silver horn in the middle of its forehead, much like the mythical unicorn. The unearthly beauty of the animal was almost lost amid the fantastic, sparkling landscape. It was a sight beyond his wildest imaginings. Everyone's eyes were transfixed at the sight of this creature. What other beings might inhabit this strange New World? They marvelled at the novel beauty and bizarreness of this island of fantastic visual delight, as do the very young when charmed and intrigued by a baby animal.

Meanwhile the natives' apprehension grew as they realized what was in store for them at the hands of their captors. They weren't going to have any of it! They would go down fighting, like men. It was now do or die. Where were they to find food and water in the abundance that they were accustomed to on their own island — the one we knew as Blackbeard's? How would they live? It might be their total undoing, needlessly costing them their lives, if they didn't defend themselves by rebelling against tyranny then and there.

Maltreatment at the hands of a few has been the bane of humanity, despite their always having been strength in numbers, as there always will be — though this is not as yet experienced by millions of people in the world. Revolts will occur eventually where there is injustice, unless the downtrodden moral and oppressed masses begin to resist the brutality and coercion. The so-called great leaders in the history books have too much blood dripping from their hands over what they have extracted from the innocents of the world.

This willingness to have others injured or killed for personal gain — whether it be for acquisition of gold doubloons, more land, or fame and fortune — is entirely wrong. People who indulge in these bloodbaths of humanity are the epitome of evil in the world and should be held to account for their sins and actions. The good people of the world should have more of a right to live in peace than anyone else who perpetrates hate for their own greed and monetary gain. Thus the world would be just and good for all.

When the natives were finally struck with the realization of the fate intended for them, spontaneous rioting broke out on deck. They started to clutch at anything and everything in sight, including buckets of water, pieces of rope, the chickens which had been left wandering on the main deck, even a wooden-staved biscuit barrel. The enraged natives started to throw every manner of item at their captors, as well as at Captains Alvarez and Salisbury. No one was exempt as the crew and officers attempted to dodge the flying missiles lobbed past their heads. Two wooden ope.

water buckets struck two of the guards in their foreheads while a third guard received a glancing blow to his temple with the biscuit barrel. They were all knocked to the ground, though not before discharging the muskets they had been clutching. One after another, they slumped to the deck like dominoes.

Meanwhile, two low-flying parrots had inadvertently been grazed by these accidental musket shots and landed on the heads of two of the unconscious guards. The birds seemed like extremely colourful feathered hats, though affording little protection from the sun. The unconscious men were unable to admire their newly acquired finery, however. Fortunately, the stunned birds had only had a few feathers missing, rendering them temporarily flightless but fully conscious and aware of their unenviable position. In screeching, high-pitched bird language, they registered their disapproval at being poised on the offending men's heads. After all, the parrots had been interrupted in their morning breakfast flight for mangoes and papayas in their special groves on the southwesterly side of the island.

Another crew member had been hit on the back of the head and knocked unconscious by a flying truncheon. The guards fell so quickly because all the debris had been thrown so accurately; the natives were accustomed to hunting for small game and were expert marksmen. Two more of the *Vigour*'s crew, now manning the *Santa Teresita*, had been knocked overboard after three large stray chickens had been scooped up by the enraged natives and thrown at them with full force. The guards, near the ropes on the port side of the main deck, had been knocked off balance as the squawking chickens sailed in their direction and past their stunned faces, flapping and slapping them in flight.

No one could fathom how the captains and crew members were going to escape from their attackers, who had used such unorthodox means to thwart their erstwhile captors. Salisbury and Alvarez were trying to come up with an escape plan, but the ongoing threat of the green people made recapture of the prisoners all but impossible. They had not envisaged a full-scale revolt, and they were themselves now at the mercy of the green islanders.

Truth be told, the island people were perfectly justified in their self-defence, just like any people in the world who are robbed, exploited and abused by the colonialists.

The rich and powerful care nothing for their subjects and slaves, whom they see only as objects to provide a means to an end. Machiavelli was right in his assessment of the elite: he was not responsible for their behaviour, but only reported and described in detail that which he observed in real life of that class of society.

Another rioting native got hold of the 'cat-of-nine-tails' occasionally used to punish errant sailors. After letting the "cat out of the bag" housing the whip, he started to crack it over his captors. The poor crewmen who were left standing, eleven in number, leapt into the air as the whip struck them with surprising accuracy on their tender buttocks. Smarting from welts inflicted liberally and with wild abandon on their *derrières*, the sailors were rapidly losing whatever advantage they still held.

The green people were going to have none of this foreign intervention, with the frightening prospect of being marooned on an inhospitable island without visible food or water. How long would they last there? A week, perhaps? It was a terrifying thought for them. It was a fight for survival and their very lives, and it would be a fight to the finish. The natives didn't know what sort of man-eating animals or other dangers might inhabit this fantasy realm, and they were in no mood to find out.

Pandemonium reigned again. Captain Salisbury's mind was temporarily paralysed with fear. He could not cope with one more blessed event, since so many difficulties, one after another in rapid succession, had beset this fateful sea voyage.

The helmsman, tired from a long shift on deck and understandably distracted by the unabated madness, bore hard to port to avoid a group of skerries — rock outcrops on the starboard side. Simultaneously though inadvertently, however, this action steered the *Santa Teresita* dangerously close to sharp rocks on the port side. Most of the crew, along with the remaining natives, were still running amok in a wild frenzy. The angry natives had captured some of the muskets, and they were now threatening the crew.

All of a sudden, the *Santa Teresita* lurched forward as we heard the sickening groan of the hull being ripped apart by one of the hundreds of foot-wide rock-finger formations along the length of the beach and its shallow waters. One of the menacing rock formations was now protruding sharply through the middle of the ship's hull, and the ship started to take on water at an alarming rate.

Had they been out to sea, instead of perched on a reef, they would have sunk into the depths of the ocean in the wink of an eye. The green people and crewmen alike screamed in panic and were preparing to jump ship immediately. They didn't have any choice now. Most of the men, white and green — it didn't matter at this point — were up to their thighs in water on the main deck. The ship was taking on water at an even greater rate and might soon be forever consigned to Neptune's briny depths.

"To the longboats! Be quick about it!" barked Salisbury, having snapped out of his trance of indecision just in the nick of time. His leadership qualities emerged, as they always did when they were put to the test.

No sooner had the hulls of the longboats touched the water than the *Santa Teresita* experienced a great shudder, and most of the hull and superstructure disappeared into the sea, generating huge waves which propelled the men to the safe refuge of the shore, virtually (and luckily) tossing them over the hundreds of sharp and dangerous protruding stones which lined the beach.

Reaching the island, the natives leapt out of their long-boats and sprinted for the sparkling waters of a natural fountain in the middle of a clearing in the dense jungle. This precious liquid quenched their parched throats. The basic necessities of life took priority over fighting. An informal truce was struck between the two opposing and warring groups, since they were all too hungry and tired to continue their pointless show of force against each other.

Tropical fruits twice the size of normal mangoes and papayas were soon found in great abundance on the leeward side of their new island home, to the great delight and relief of everyone that their fears had been groundless. Indeed, there was enough food to feed a small army of hungry men on their tiny corner of tropical paradise. Everyone was soon satiated with the abundant food and liquid after greedily feasting and drinking from the bright pink, turquoise and gold coloured fruits.

The new inhabitants proceeded to make camp in their respective areas of the beach and jungle; it was a moonless night, and their fires were burning low. The sailors chose to sleep on the pink sand. The natives, on the other hand, preferred the palm leaves strewn in wild abandon on a beach on the opposite side of the island.

A night watch of two men was set up by each of the camps to monitor any perceived threat from the other camp. The snoring from both camps resounded and echoed from beach to beach and in the jungle. The loudness probably kept the parrots awake at night, and I imagined them pacing back and forth on their roosting branches, hoping to catch a few winks of sleep.

Thoughts of domesticity centre the mind so that we may again go about our business without anxiety, nervousness and worry. Going back to the warmth and security of our families, relations, and close friends, we may again revive our flagging spirits and hearts, once more to be filled like empty vessels with the human essence of life.

All these adventures and mishaps had, though not through my fault, driven a wedge of distance between my family and myself. I wished with all my heart to be comforted by my kind mother. I knew not in my heart of hearts if I should see her again, considering the dire circumstances the captains and crews had been finding themselves in over and over again. Wondering if this voyage would ever end, I shed a quiet tear at the thought of my situation here, far from home and at the mercy of nature and her elements, with a few restless natives thrown in for good measure to keep the pot boiling.

In the tranquillity of the next morning, the sailors found, to their great relief, that the *Santa Teresita* was now safely beached at low tide and was relatively unscathed — damaged but reparable — after having being virtually sunk the night before. They would not have had any other means of escape from the island without the ship, since the longboats were not seaworthy on the open sea. Alvarez's ship would have to be careened and refitted, since she had sustained major damage in the storm. This otherwise unfortunate turn of events proved, however, to be a blessing in disguise.

14. Repairing the *Santa Teresita*

NIGHT FELL QUICKLY on the tropical isle. Four sentries would be placed on the night watch instead of the usual two, for greater safety and security. A full moon made their task easier as the crewmen dipped their oars into the warm waters of the Pacific Ocean for the last time that evening.

With both ships finally secured and the day's work behind them, Salisbury was finally was able to lay his exhausted head on a sea-grass pillow rolled into his coat for a well-deserved sleep. Salisbury was tired to the depths of his heart and soul. He, too, yearned to see his beloved wife and infant daughter. Lost in reverie in a rare moment of silence on the island, he imagined himself missing his daughter's first baby steps. He was filled with longing and sadness at the thought of them, wishing to be transported home at once to experience his family hearth's warmth again, even if only briefly.

Captain Alvarez, already snoring loudly, lay covered with a few palm leaves. The majority of the men slept in rows on the beach without any blankets, since the sand still radiated warmth from the broiling sun, which had beat down on them for so many days now. Some crewmen slept in hammocks slung between two palm trees. Everyone settled down for the night, including the baboons and apes. Their loud calls and ranting dissipated into the warm, pleasant evening air by dusk. The full moon rose in the sky, and the whole island was illuminated with the palm trees silhouetted on the beach and swaying to the gentle breeze.

On the morning of the next day, the captains Salisbury and Alvarez had lengthy discussions on how the repairs and careening were supposed to be done and what length of time would be required for all the work, as well as what other tasks the men would be required to do to complete the job.

William Bartlesby, our ship's talented master carpenter, along with both the carpenter's helper and Simon Crudgely, our new baker and cook, were ordered by Captain Salisbury to make the required labour-intensive preparations to commence repairs on the ship without delay. Three other crew members were also recruited to help in this time-consuming endeavour. Repairs were likely to take the better part of a fortnight, even working round the clock, before we could set sail again for England.

Mr. Bartlesby was teaching his helper the craft of ship-building and ship repair. This included, for instance, instructing the lad on choosing the truest and straightest trees to fell, which were essential to replace the mainmast that had been snapped with the gale force of winds and waves. Three teak trees were subsequently felled by the carpenter's assistants, stout and hardy farm lads from Kent and Cambridgeshire — with Simon observing them, keen to learn under the tutelage of the ship's master carpenter and the other more experienced hands. Masts

and lines were replaced at breakneck speed, since work repairs
were being made round the clock. Rotating crews of workmen
caulked the shrinking planks and floorboards with oakum and
tar brushes to make the *Vigour* seaworthy.

Truth be told, young Simon was becoming more and more
homesick by the day. Much like myself, he missed his mother who
had only sent him to sea — much against her kind and tender
maternal wishes — when finances (or the lack thereof) required
it, as is the way with most people of this unequal, unjust world.
Unbidden thoughts of her brought tears to his young eyes. The
stocky lad longed to be at home, reunited with his parents. He
pictured himself sitting in front of the open fireplace on his stool
beside his reassuring mother, quietly darning socks, humming
softly while rocking his baby sister in her cradle on the floor by
her foot. He also dreamed of marriage to a village girl he knew
back home.

Meanwhile, the natives had been granted the use of the
ship's dinghy and, with free rein of the island, they hunted for
food and set up camp on the leeward side. With their newfound
freedom, they aided Alvarez and the other crew members in
gathering provisions for the homeward voyage. They foraged for
food before we were awake, and brought us papayas, mangoes
and starfruit, along with breadfruit baked in underground ovens,
as a peace offering. They dried breadfruit, mangoes and papayas
in the sun, and salted barrels of boar meat. They captured hapless
turtles, some of which were eventually presented as exotic gifts to
the king and queen of England. Some of the Captain's men were

to see these turtles years later in the royal gardens in Windsor after their final voyage home.

The green people were generous, helpful and kind-hearted, not only because of their closeness to nature but also because they wanted to be rid of their uninvited "guests" who had, from their point of view, turned into the largest pests ever to inhabit these islands. No doubt the locals wanted peace and quiet restored to their tropical paradise as soon and possible.

The Green and Black Lads, as the work crew's additional hundred or so native people were somewhat affectionately but respectfully known by the regular crew, soon became voluntary able-bodied seamen in their own right. In this case, many hands did make the work lighter, as the saying went. A few of them now sported soiled neckerchiefs, given them by appreciative sailors, to keep their tousled dreadlocks from becoming tarred as they worked on the hull of the ship.

They assisted Mr. Bartlesby willingly and even cheerfully, realizing that their own chances of getting off the island depended on cooperation with the ship's carpenter and his assistants, as well as with all the people who had been aboard the *Vigour*. Without the help of all these people, they would be stuck on this minuscule island. While both groups were still learning each other's language, they had devised a combination of hand gestures and pidgin words to better understood each other.

The quartermaster sent two sailors with wooden buckets and kegs, as well as copper pots from the galley, to replenish the ships' water barrels by rowing the longboat to the point on the beach where the water downstream of the waterfall rushed into the ocean. The place they chose was only about 400 paces from the falls, a subtropical setting with crimson and yellow hibiscus flowers abounding with flourishes of bird of paradise and orchids of delicate mauve and pink hues dripping from branches of fruit trees and nut trees. The whole jungle was sheltered by huge palms that waved gently in the mid-afternoon heat. The scene was worthy of the finest painter in England.

The young men were overcome by the beauty of the place and might have remained there indefinitely to savour the moment, but duty and necessity called them. They filled the wooden buckets and copper pots with the pure, crystalline waters that thundered down the cliff, then positioned the containers with care in their rowboat, alternating left and right, proceeding from both fore and aft towards the middle, all done in order to keep the boat balanced in the sea.

After about half an hour of carrying their precious liquid to their longboat, they felt the small boat could not safely carry any more water and still be kept safe from capsizing, so they ferried their supply back, raised it aboard the ship with the aid of deck cranes and poured it into the larger shipboard casks. They repeated this water re-supplying operation several times, until the quartermaster was satisfied that the stock of water stored on the *Santa Teresita* was now adequate for their ship and that there was sufficient in reserve to be able to resupply the *Vigour* later as well.

Meanwhile, the men set about their tasks of securing the other supplies. The site was a beehive of activity, with the men being sent back and forth to secure supplies to re-plank parts of the hull and to re-caulk it with oakum and tar. Three fires were set with tinderboxes and flint beneath the tar pots, using sea grass and tangled twigs from low scrub bushes on the hill overlooking the beach. The open flame brought the black, thick, sticky liquid to a rolling, sputtering boil.

On the beach, huge pots, axes and crowbars were brought out from the ship by the overworked, overwrought, perspiring crew. This ship had been painstakingly dragged to the safe higher ground and braced by beams, like the flying buttresses on a great Gothic cathedral. With the *Santa Teresita* perched on this sturdy scaffolding beneath the fore and aft of the hull, it was safe for us to work next to the ship without fear of its tipping over and crushing us.

The crew hauled out tar pots, heated up the sticky mixture and sealed leaks between the planks with rope or rag or whatever bric-a-brac was at hand, and then tarred them with a steady brush. Other planks had to be removed and replaced before sealing with the coating that would protect them from the worst effects of the sea. Making the ship seaworthy was labour which could only be done with trained, experienced sea hands.

The living quarters — now waterlogged, damp, unhealthy and musty from constant exposure to the seas for months at a time — were thoroughly scrubbed with vinegar to remove the mould on the walls of the ship and to freshen the fetid air. Our Captain Salisbury knew of the risk of general malady or even consumption overtaking the men as an occupational hazard in the seafaring way of life. Salisbury's concern for his seamen was wholly admirable, and I am certain he did much to protect their health and increase their life span — pitiable sailors who before this time had been treated most poorly and cruelly, almost as an expendable commodity by their officers.

The success or failure of all voyages depended utterly on the sailors, who did all the physical labour required for the smooth running of a ship. Seasoned naval personnel were hard to come by. A missing crewman could prove disastrous to the entire voyage, since his physical work was important and the slack could not always be taken up by all the other crew members, constantly busy as they were themselves. In addition to being a caring and intelligent leader of his men, Salisbury had read widely and applied his learning to help keep him and his fellow officers and sailors strong and healthy. He was held in high esteem by all his colleagues and crew members alike for his enlightened and educated mind and his natural kindness of personality. Not a single man had been lost to scurvy or sickness either on this expedition or on his previous one, and he wanted no one to perish if he could do anything to prevent it.

The job of the sailing man was fraught with danger at every turn and was physically demanding. It required precision timing when handling the sails, as well as agility in climbing the rope ladders to adjust the rigging lines, especially when their ship was being battered and tossed about by 60-foot waves in the middle of a typhoon. Many a man had sometimes had to be lashed to the rigging to avoid suffering the same fate of being washed away to sea, as many others on other ships already had been. The swelling of the waves in stormy weather caused the ship to almost capsize with every sharp gust of wind. The sea is the most powerful element in nature and must be treated with respect and caution at every turn. They had to weather the storm while facing great danger to their personal safety and that of their fellow crew members.

15. A dangerous encounter

THE CAPTAIN'S MEDITATIONS were interrupted one morning by the sound of far-off voices in the east, which seemed to be talking gibberish or ranting loudly in a foreign language. Salisbury muttered to himself about the rude interruption. He had been attempting to keep up his appearance by shaving with a straight razor under a shading palm tree. The sun's rays were warm even at that time of day, it being the summer season. He had risen early so as to dress, shave and gather his thoughts for the day before the others arose. He needed to plan the next course of action for all his crew, passengers and fellow officers in his charge.

The unknown voices became gradually louder and louder, and he worried they might be approaching his camp. Salisbury alerted the sentries as to his intention and stealthily approached the direction of the voices. As he came closer, he could make out the distinct gliding sibilants of people loudly conversing in Portuguese. Captain Salisbury understood the rudiments of this language, since he had received some of his naval training as a lad on a Portuguese vessel, after having been kidnapped from his mother's side when his family was travelling to Spain. He had escaped from his captors only after seven years. The sound of their voices caused fear and loathing in his heart, but he had to deal with the immediacy of the situation at hand and to overlook his past experiences.

"Parem de discutir imediatamente, insensatos! Ou eu vou bater a cabeça em conjunto!" the unknown leader of these rather unsavoury wretches hissed. Salisbury understood that one man was threatening two others who had been arguing.

"Polly don't like it when you 'it her on the 'ead with a bananee!" a distinct Yorkshire voice chimed in.

Captain Salisbury was startled to hear this English voice amongst the Portuguese. "Don't make any more noise, or they'll shoot us!" the raspy voice further warned them.

Captain Salisbury returned to his own encampment, quickly roused Captain Alvarez and his officers and men from their slumber on the beach where they had remained that night to provide protection for their group. Salisbury and his men hushed the officers to keep them from alerting the interlopers, then whispered and gestured to explain his plan of action. Higgles and McCaffrey were sent to quietly rouse the rest of the crew.

They would have to ambush and overpower their would-be attackers before the rogues were able to inflict any injury on his own men and those of Captain Alvarez. The unknown individuals were now apparently approaching their makeshift encampment in earnest, and the volume of their voices was increasing. The officers did not know the number of attackers they would be encountering — without proper armaments and with their backs to the sea. Captain Salisbury promised himself that henceforth, and for the remainder of the voyage, if he could just scrape through this looming predicament, he would arm his men to the teeth and keep the muskets primed and loaded to ensure their safety against any sneak attack. This "wisdom of hindsight" was forever emblazoned in his brain.

Besides the longboat, there seemed no escape route other than swimming back to the *Vigour* or the *Santa Teresita*. Three-quarters of the Spanish men did not possess this aquatic skill, however. Salisbury silently vowed to make sure that as soon as the emergency was over, all the sailors would learn how to swim and master the art by the end of this voyage.

"Take four of our crew. That's all we can spare now," Salisbury ordered in terse, direct military tones. "Row out the longboat and pick up muskets and gunpowder for 90 men. The men must launch their longboat from the sheltered bay on the northwest side of the island," he said emphatically, "even though the waters may be treacherous. We'll be detected otherwise."

"It's our only hope. We will be at the mercy of these foul strangers, depending upon their numbers," he said, obviously deeply worried. "We'll have to take that chance. It's the only way we'll be able to get to our muskets and ammunition, since the longboat will be intercepted immediately if we launch them here in broad daylight from such a visible point."

The muskets and ammunition had not been loaded into the longboat the night before, since darkness had fallen soon after our arrival. We were only able to begin transporting the male adult passengers in mid-morning after ferrying the men, the

food and other supplies to their new temporary home in order
that their women and children could remain in the safety of the
ships. There wasn't enough space for all the people on the ships
to sleep comfortably. The decks of all the ships were, as usual,
quite overcrowded and overrun with the extra passengers. It was
pandemonium with the teeming masses.

"Ready our men as best we can here, Mr. Sullivan,"
Captain Salisbury ordered his first mate. "Send the remaining
sentries on a surveillance mission to determine how many armed
men there are." It sounded like the mysterious voices were fast
approaching their camp. Salisbury and Alvarez braced themselves
for the worst, motioning the men to scatter into the jungle and
hide behind the luxuriant vegetation. There they might at least
surprise, surround and capture their intruders, if nothing else.

The mystery people came closer, but Captain Salisbury
still could not determine the number, since only their voices
carried in the hot, tropical air.

"I explicitly told everyone to remain on the westerly
part of this island until we were able to spare a few groups of
men to explore the whole circumference of the island! Safety
in numbers!" he angrily muttered, at the unbidden thought of
his men disobeying his express orders and putting everyone in
immediate danger. The oppressive, humid air did nothing to
improve Salisbury's humour.

Though the sentries had left with much trepidation, they
returned from their scouting mission looking incredulous at
what they had found. To their astonishment, they found only ten
deranged-looking, bedraggled and ranting individuals, though
in the forest while arguing they had sounded like a group of

anywhere from 50 to a hundred. On questioning, Salisbury determined that the ragtag group had employed many voices, accents and manners of speaking — 200 all told — to keep themselves amused and entertained over the years they had lived on the island in virtual isolation from the world. They had tried to escape from the island a few times, but their primitive boats, rafts and dugouts proved unworthy to withstand the treacherous tides which surrounded the island or sail the distances required to reach the nearest inhabited land. Indeed, much of the wood from the island's trees was unusually porous, and their unseaworthy rafts had quickly become waterlogged. They'd had to swim back, unsuccessful at making their escape, on numerous occasions.

Fortunately for them, a few wild goats had formed the nucleus of a captive herd, which furnished them with fresh milk, cheese and meat. The crew, who'd formerly been pressed into sailing with privateers, subsequently became goatherds, from sheer necessity. It was, admittedly, easier than a pirate's life by far. Along the way, they also learned to distil and imbibe rum, since sugar cane was native to this island and was cultivated in even greater quantities on the southeast part of the island, which had higher rainfalls. The men shared some of their liquor, which they stored in gourds clutched in their hands, with their newfound "guests" from the *Vigour* and the *Santa Teresita*.

This group of privateers-turned-goatherds were the nearest we had come to finding pirates on our voyage in search of fabled treasure, or so we thought.

Again we set sail, our ships now repaired, and knowing that a state of relative peace existed between us and our various counterparts, whether human or ape. When both the *Vigour* and the *Santa Teresita* reached Blackbeard's Island, we breathed a collective sigh of relief, and our spirits were revived with the anticipation of fresh water and food. The *Vigour* glided across the azure waters, and crew and Captain were busy scurrying aboard the ship performing the tasks needed to make ready to disembark after our last days at sea. The men were anxious to walk on dry land again to give their sea legs a rest.

Again, we were met with unfamiliar sights and sounds, after rowing the longboat ashore on this island abundant with palm trees. Turtles too numerous to count swam freely in the turquoise waters of a sheltered lagoon. I was initially fearful that our men might be attacked by these voracious-seeming creatures, since they appeared to demonstrate no fear of man. Indeed, humans were only a novelty to these amphibians and a source of interest and curiosity to them. The weight of these giant, carefree swimmers ranged from five to ten stone.

When the men in their longboats reached the easterly side of Blackbeard's Island, they proceeded to shoot wild boar with ball and musket, laying out the meat in strips on makeshift racks to dry in the hot tropical sun. They gathered fruits, nuts and wild vegetables of every description and colour — all of which, of course, had been identified first by Dr. Loyster to ensure they were edible and not poisonous. By watching what the monkeys ate, he identified several varieties of new fruits which he deemed to be edible and delicious after sampling them. Another plant was quite bitter raw, but he had encountered this plant before, and told the men that they must boil the root, changing the water three times during the boiling, to leach out the bitterness.

Meanwhile, the ship's botanist catalogued — and planned to transport — hundreds of new specimens of flora and fauna that he had discovered on the fertile and lush tropical island. These eventually found their way back to England, where they were cared for by the royal gardener Charles Bridgman, before forming the heart of the botanical collection recently established by Princess Augusta and Lord Bute in their new conservatory at Kew Gardens.

The men were enthralled and entranced, to the point that they failed to notice two beady eyes staring at them through the jungle underbrush, set back from the beach about a hundred paces. The shores and sands of the island seemed to welcome them with a warm hospitality. They were, however, justifiably hesitant to slip into a state of total tranquillity. They were on their guard, their senses sharpened for survival.

Captain Salisbury had, however, suspected that a plot was afoot, because the island seemed so quiet. On first approach, the ship's lookout had spotted a wisp of smoke through his spyglass. It had appeared to been recently extinguished — perhaps in a futile bid to avoid detection, or perhaps to lure him and his crew into a false sense of security.

When, after his long self-imposed absence, I chanced, whilst on a walk through a wooded glen, to hear Ishmael Kratz' voice again, I fairly jumped out of my skin. I heard him say: "Aye, lads." I was dumbfounded, and terror seized me by the throat. My breath was stifled and I fairly fell to the ground on my knees. How could it be? Was he on Blackbeard's Island, too? Terror filled my very soul at the prospect of again meeting Kratz face to face, and I took care to remain concealed. He was to me the very embodiment of evil, magnified by the knowledge of his previous treachery. In the middle of a heated exchange, Kratz flew into an even greater rage, and he attacked one of his men mercilessly, aiming blows at the unfortunate man's head.

"Take that, ye thievin' blaggard," hissed Kratz, as he struck the crew member about the head and shoulders with his closed fists. "I'll larn ye to pilfer from me," he continued, while still delivering blows to the offending pirate. It was justice pirate-style: swift, cruel and unpredictable. The beaten man's eyes glowered with a sullen desire for revenge. I was sure I would be spotted by the pirate band, but it was most fortunately not to be. They continued on their journey, and the loud recriminations continued as well.

I hurried back to alert Captain Salisbury, and he quickly hatched an ingenious plan. While the pirates were seeking treasure on the island, he would sail around the island with two longboats to surprise the *Contessa* where she lay anchored. There would only be a small number of people left aboard, he felt sure, as the pirates were greedily anxious to find the treasure, or at least the portion of it, that Blackbeard was supposed to have buried on this island.

Our longboat men rowed, dipping their oars quietly into the waters. They did not wish to arouse any suspicions or warn the pirates of their presence, in case they had left some sentries to guard the *Contessa*. We could hear the pirates' voices as the belligerent exchanges of two somewhat drunken sailors floated through the air, and the words became more and more slurred the closer the longboats approached. Once again, rum was taking its toll on this motley crew of disheveled individuals. As the boats glided closer to the pirate ship, it became more and more evident that no one on board was guarding the vessel. There was no one on deck; perhaps the pirates really had not anticipated any uninvited "guests" on this remote island in the middle of the seven seas. To their knowledge, they were the only keepers of the map of Blackbeard's Island. After Kratz had stolen the original map, they thought they were the only ones in the world who knew of the island's great treasure and its likely whereabouts.

Only the creaking of the heavy timbers of the ship's hull and the gentle lapping of the waves on the bow could be heard when the men from the *Vigour* boarded the pirate vessel. They moved stealthily, like cats in the night, to avoid detection. The Captain ordered the men to board the ship and try to overpower any of the sleeping or inebriated buccaneers so that they could take charge of the ship. Perhaps their vessel, too, had a valuable cargo like stolen doubloons, jewels, gold or silver bullion from South America; spices, tea or teak lumber from the jungles of the Amazon; or rum and cones of sugar from the Caribbean.

As the longboats nudged the starboard side of the vessel, the crew of the *Vigour* drew their knives and clenched them between their teeth. They checked their muskets for powder and ball. A hooked sisal ladder had been thrown hastily over the midships. The men from the *Vigour*, upon reaching the ladder, steadied their boats as they picked their way, cautiously and quietly climbing up the rope ladder to slip onto the ship's deck. With the moon beginning to rise, they hoped to maintain the advantage of surprise and to avoid detection by any crew members who might had been left on deck to guard the *Contessa*.

The pirate ship had a ghostly, derelict appearance. Its tattered sails were silhouetted by the moon, which spooked the already apprehensive crew of the *Vigour*. They spoke barely above a whisper, so as not to arouse the suspicions of any pirate who may have been left aboard.

As each crew member reached the top of the ladder, he stepped barefoot on the deck so as not to be heard and alert any pirates. The plan was executed with near-clockwork precision. I observed no lanterns lit on the deck or in the forecastle. Perhaps they were sleeping below.

But the Captain soon found one of the pirates.

"You'd better clap your trap if you want to see another day or another dram of rum, you blaggard!" Captain Salisbury hissed into his victim's ear, his arm around the captured pirate's brown, leathery, sweaty neck — all the while covering his mouth with his hand lest the pirate summon the rest of his drunken, motley crew with a warning cry.

"'Oo're you?" the man croaked with a shaky voice, quite immobilized with fear after being accosted. From deck to deck they went, searching for pirates in their sleeping quarters or anyplace else where they could have concealed themselves. A second pirate was spotted in the moonlight sleeping on his watch sprawled out on the deck next to the ships' wheel. As he awoke, he swore an oath at the Captain, "I'll run ye through, ye blaggard, if ye don't step aside." Marvell Dickins, a crewman from the *Vigour*, however, had quietly crept up behind him, forced him to drop his sword and clapped his hand over the pirate's mouth so he could not alert any other pirates who might yet be on board and awaiting discovery.

We talked in whispers. We would have to capture the rest of the pirate crew, having no idea of their actual numbers. As it turned out, however, the pirates had left only those two of their number behind on guard duty, which task they had so spectacularly failed at, so we now had full control of the ship, with "guards" under arrest. The ship turned out to be utterly devoid of wealth; perhaps they had already spirited off their ill-gotten gains to elsewhere.

Since our Captain possessed a second copy of Blackbeard's map, he knew precisely the location on Blackbeard's Island where Kratz and his men would be bound for. We had only to lie in wait near the marked place, where the pirate band had already begun digging a hole. They dug in several places, but their search was fruitless. Whatever gold might have been there once was evidently there no longer. We lay in wait till all the frustrated thieves had fallen asleep, and we were able to take the lot of them by surprise.

Captain Alvarez clapped the captives in irons. He even recognized several of them from a raid on a ship that he had sailed on years earlier, before assuming command of his present ship, and he vowed to bring them to justice in Spain for their crimes.

Now with three good ships, we had room for all the crew members and passengers. The men readied the rigging of the *Vigour* for the return sail to England, while the *Santa Teresita* and the *Contessa* were to sail for Spain. In another month we would be home with our families and loved ones — or we would have been, except for one fateful surprise which Captain Alvarez still had in store for us all.

16. Home again in England

I DIDN'T KNOW MUCH ABOUT THIS during the time I served as a cabin boy on the *Vigour,* and still less at the time that I was helping my mother at the White Horse Inn, but in the 1500s, when Spain was at the zenith of her naval power, hundreds of galleons, laden with heavy gold and silver treasure stolen from the Inca civilization in South America, had sunk. This was due to their unstable design; the rudder was disproportionate to the overall size of the ship, adversely affecting their manœuvrability. The Spanish also tended to mount too many cannons aboard, which, being placed relatively high to provide adequate firing distance, tended to make the ships top-heavy.

The Spanish then compounded the design flaws of their ships and munitions practices by making it a habit of overloading with too much treasure on each trip, since there was so much to be taken from the Incan world — gold bullion and plate by the ton. To be sure, without the cannons they might have proved an even more tempting target for piracy, and without the gold they would not have been able to provide Spain with the wealth to build her famous Armada, which was so soundly defeated by the English fleet more than a century before I was born.

Captain Juan Alvarez had once researched these sunken ships at the museum and archives in Madrid where the detailed ship records were kept. He had determined that many of these ships had foundered close to shore, since the heavy treasure which had been piled high on the decks had contributed even more to the instability of the already unstable craft, causing them to sink with great loss to crew and officers, especially as many of them had come from landlocked villages in the farming regions of their country; unfortunately for them, few actually knew how to swim.

One such great ship, the *Alba*, had foundered and had sunk quite close to a group of islands known as the Azores. The officers, who were from many different countries, had thought it was beneath the dignity of their aristocracy to expend the effort to actually learn much about seamanship. Like other galleons of her type, the *Alba* shared a basically unstable design, which caused it to capsize in a rather insignificant storm. The men on deck had watched in horror as the Spanish galleon had listed and then was swamped with waves that slapped them to and fro, like toy boats upon a lily pond. Most of the crew had drowned after thrashing about in the waters.

Captain Alvarez had made a very accurate chart of where the ship had been wrecked some 150 years earlier. With the aid of this carefully researched chart, we all were to become wealthy later — by helping the crew of the *Santa Teresita* in salvaging the gold that had been piled high on the deck of the sunken *Alba*.

Recovering a substantial portion of the treasure lost in the ship's sinking eventually became a major salvaging operation for Captain Salisbury, who employed our heavy diving bell. The bell was a device known to the Greek philosopher Aristotle, but its design had been recently improved on by the former Royal Navy captain and astronomer Edmond Halley. (He was the scientist who first theorized that the comets regularly visible in our skies every 75 years or so were, in reality, recurrent appearances of the very same comet.)

With possession of that treasure, the crew and captain alike, had they been so inclined, could have rolled about to their hearts' content in gold doubloons and pieces-of-eight for the rest of their lives. They were wealthy now beyond their wildest dreams. The treasure we had recovered from the sunken *Alba* was equally divided among the entire crew and passengers, with not even the captains claiming a greater share of the booty.

Despite our captain's attentive care for the health of his crew, not all survived our voyage; shares were allotted for the souls lost at sea, to take care both of those who had returned and of the families of those who did not. Our crew were able to help their families and those in need in England, establishing alms-houses and good schools for the poor families of the crew who had not returned from the voyage to Blackbeard's Island. England — nay, all of Europe, what with the joyous and heartfelt receptions offered to the Spaniards and other Europeans — was a merrier and happier place because of the efforts and generosity of the captains and, of course, their dedicated, reliable and hard-working crews.

Because the *Alba* never returned to Cadiz with its treasure and bullion, the Spanish authorities had assumed she had been lost at sea. In due course of time, Spain sent out a search party to locate the ship and her treasure, but they had no luck, since unlike our captain, they did not know the exact location of the sinking. When the Spaniards searched, they found people who had heard of a ship's taking on treasure, but they found no one who had seen our salvage operation and would speak of it. Neither other sailors nor longshoremen, even when plied with drink, could provide information, and the Spanish never succeeded in reclaiming from us any of their hoard of treasure. Fortunately for us, the trail had gone cold.

All the mariners on the voyage had been sworn to secrecy as to what had transpired, but as the sailors I sailed with are now mostly passed on into the next world, and as this book is written many years after the events occurred, and in English, I feel relatively safe that I will injure no one by writing it down now for the sake of my children and, eventually, grandchildren.

On our return to England from our seafaring trip, we also learned than the sallow, lecherous Lord Dunston had died some months previously. At the end, having no legitimate heir to inherit his vast properties, he had then attempted to redeem himself for his wicked life by leaving his accumulated wealth, as well as his manor home and estates, to our Simon Crudgely.

Simon married a pleasant, good-hearted and generous country woman, and the two of them invited his parents Albert and Edwina Crudgely to live with them, wanting in some way to help right the wrongs that had been inflicted on his mother.

Simon's good-natured parents declined this generous invitation, so instead Simon — good son that he was, and now wealthy from his ownership of bakeries in Canterbury, Salisbury and Cambridge — had a half-timbered village house built for them that resembled Shakespeare's Tudor dwelling in Stratford-on-Avon. King George even developed a fancy for the hot cross buns and made them popular at court. Young Simon could scarcely keep up with demand and became a very wealthy man, partly with the proceeds of his yearly task of providing the royal court and with a stock of these much-enjoyed buns, which became a royal tradition.

Beginning in 1750, wealthy landowners prevailed upon political allies in Parliament to pass a series of Enclosure Acts. These punitive laws, forcing landless tenant farmers off cropland that had previously been held in common for the community, demonstrated that aristocracy cared more for sheep's wool than for the lives of tenants now dying of starvation. Indeed, the landed gentry and aristocrats had decided to feed sheep instead of people.

The sufferings of the poor were of little or no concern to the mindless pleasure-seeking aristocrats and merchant classes who tended to occupy themselves with trivial matters. From riding habits to tea dresses, women spent much time on their toilette, changing costumes as many as five times a day, while their foppish menfolk engaged in mindless pursuits of pleasures — learning to strut with a commanding bearing like landed gentry, gambling, pleasantries and conquests over servants. Their trivial behaviour was at the expense of hard-working peasants who provided food and luxuries for the wealthy so that the latter could prance around their estates engaged in pointless dalliances. These unequivocal and original ne'er-do-wells were totally dependent upon their labouring serfs, tenant farmers and household staff.

The oppression of the majority by the undeserving tyranny of a few, of course, has probably happened since the very dawn of civilization, and has been our history for too long. Too hungry to revolt against tyranny, the peasants died instead from exhaustion and starvation, while the clergy in little village churches assured them of their reward in heaven. Somehow the "deserving" on earth turned out to be — mistakenly, of course — not those who produced the very food that fed them, who built the grand homes that housed them or who waited on these ingrates hand and foot.

Many a clever peasant must occasionally have wondered why the rich and wealthy seemed to have received their "reward" on earth, especially since the peasant was producing this reward for them. Why, the peasant again might have wondered, did the lord receive the majority of the fruits of his servants' hard labours? For the most part, the landowners were wasteful and abusive to the peasants feeding them. The conundrum was not answered in fairness for the struggling tenant farmers forced to ignore their own wishes and desires while their oppressors — lords, kings, and whoever and whatever — grow fatter and wealthier at their expense.

Wars and conflicts since the beginning of time were fought not for the benefit of those who have the most to lose — innocent children, women and men. Only when a country must defend itself from unwarranted and unprovoked aggression need force be used to protect itself and its citizens. When people in control think to benefit at the cost of the blood and dead bodies of a country's citizens, they pervert its nation's children to kill other innocent people in other lands — an action which does not come naturally to human beings, who for the most part can live in harmony. War is for the rich who benefit by providing equipment and who acquire lands or natural resources or other spoils of "victory." Generally, all grand and great buildings of the past and present are built with blood on the hands of their owners. They are, in fact, a tribute to the hard-working hands and bodies of the general, unsung and insufficiently glorified labourers — beasts of burden for the rich whose only power is taken from the majority of people in society.

There is only power of the rich if it is over the poor. The people united can overthrow tyranny, because the governments of the world do not have jails big enough to put in hundreds of millions of people. Power, control by governments — kings, queens and presidents — is only superficial. The elites have only as much power and control as is given to them by the masses. The leaders fear unity and peace, which can defeat the most cruel tyrant; the meek will inherit the earth — that is, what is left of it.

Simon was eventually able to offer employment to some of the many rural workers who had been dispossessed and had fallen upon hard times after parliamentary passage of the notorious Enclosure Acts had ruined their livelihood. Thus it was that Simon, through goodness and kindness, helped to avenge the maltreatment of his mother at the hands of the cruel and inhuman lord. Simon always believed in his young mind, just as the vicar had preached at the village church: "As ye sow, so shall ye reap." Dunston's death and Simon's life truly demonstrated and bore out this biblical saying. Young Simon and his now white-haired mother were at last reaping their just rewards.

Following the excellent example of Captain Salisbury, I eventually became a sea captain myself and sailed many voyages, but I have no space to recount these here. I have, of course, kept some detailed journals from my later voyages, and I may relate them during the years to come. I am now too old to sail the seas, but I have not abandoned the seagoing life altogether, as I nowadays sail a barge on the Thames. My little crew consists of my wife, Mabel, two sons and a daughter.

Mabel is a famed midwife who ably tends to the injured or sick whom we may encounter from time to time. She has safely delivered many babies, and she is proud to say that of the many women she has attended in their confinement, she has not lost one mother to childbed fever, a fact which she attributes to her scrupulous good hygiene.

Pirates now seem to be pretty much a thing of the past, and I have given up the drinking of rum, a habit I unfortunately began very early in my sailing career. I have noticed many good sailors brought low by the ravages of excessive drink. Now, in the person of my good wife, I have the welcome attention of a sympathetic friend and helpmate to keep me civil. At another time I may recount my sea adventures in the Tortugas and elsewhere.

THE END